WESTERN HONEYMOON TREK

WESTERN HONEYMOON TREK

AS TOLD BY BRAVE HAWK

DonD Sylvain

Ordering Information:

For orders and inquiries, please contact:
1-888-375-9818
www.toplinkpublishing.com
bookorder@toplinkpublishing.com

Printed in the United States of America

WESTERN HONEYMOON TREK

AS TOLD BY BRAVE HAWK

Aunt Sue and the girls were anxious to get started on our trip to the West. Chum asked us to wait he had to make a trip to the trading post. He would go that far with us. The girls were still working on sorting out the things that they would actually need. Soap and toiletries were one of their big concerns. Told them they would need both light and heavy clothing.

Sue and mom had made up different blankets with goose down for comfort. Could fold over and lay on top of or cover-up in side the folds. Mom said if she was younger she would go, but someone needed to stay and take care of the farm. We all knew that she didn't really want to go. It wasn't long we would be on our way.

Was making up my mind what horses we would take. We had a very good selection to choose from my mare had two colts born, both males. I road both now to get them used to my ways, they both responded well. My mare had establish herself as head of the herd. We had one other mare very good animal but was always challenging my mare. Mom had wanted me to take her, decided not to she would cause too much trouble with her constant challenge to my mare. The two colts were now young horse spirited but controllable.

Decided to take 10 horses in all, this made for light load for all. Also if we were to lose one of our horses we would have extra to fall back on. We would go to our trading post first. Chum was coming as far as the trading post, the girls had not seen it as yet. He was bringing supplies and bringing back the hides that we were trading for. We were still doing quite well with our trading. Did our best not to cheat the Indians. We heard about other posts that were trading in whiskey. We still wouldn't use whiskey even though some still asked for it.

The men running the post would welcome new supplies and extra goodies we brought with us. Our trip was about ready to start. We waited for the spring flooding to subside then we would start. Everyone is anxious to get started, I just wanted it to be as safe as possible. Finally the day arrived. We made the rounds to say our goodbyes. We were wishing Godspeed and good luck, quite a few said they wish that they were going. Some of the girls made comments how fortunate we were to be able to go. They asked how long would we be gone. My answer was we would be back just before fall. 3 to 4 months in all. We would be in the wilderness all the time.

We started off without a hitch. The only problem was the girls getting used to riding all day long. The first night was a lot of moaning but in good spirits. The next few days had everyone walk beside the horses to limber up. I did the same. Chum was ahead of us with the other men and the carts. The trail by now was well defined. Most bad places had been circumvented to make it easier going. Slow getting started in the morning, the routine had not been set as yet. Be a couple of weeks or more before he would settle into a good routine.

Chum always came back and stayed with us in the evening. He got a big charge out of the girls moaning. All I could say is that they would toughen up in just a few days, everyone was in good spirits. Once in a while there would be some stumbling we all got a laugh over. Everyone was sleeping soundly, was relying on my dog for anything that might show up to cause us a problem. The deer along the trail were learning to stay clear being shot at and one of them going down. The rifle's crack had let them know that not safe when they hear men coming.

By the time we arrived at this trading post everyone was over the stiff and sore muscles. We still walked with the horses just to keep the legs in good shape. Jan and I occasionally would take off on a run. We both enjoyed the exercise, Bess and Guy were satisfied with walking with the horses Sue did the same. We stayed at the trading Post for a few days. I was hoping to see some of my Indian family. Other Indians showed up asked them if they had seen any of my family. They told me they hadn't seen them in many moons, I thought this very unusual.

Told the gang we would find a village in a week or so. Chum and Sue said their goodbyes. Chum asking Sue if she wanted to continue or go back with him. Sue answered that she would never have another chance like this if he didn't mind she would continue. I knew they would like the Black Hills the Badlands we would circumvent. We took our time and made camp early. Next morning we were on our way early. About mid morning, I kept getting an uneasy feeling. Told the gang was going to leave on foot and to keep my mare with you. Will take my dog and scout back along the trail. Felt we were being followed.

Took off on a trot and left the trail and would come to a rise being careful not to let myself be seen. Sure enough four men were following. Headed back to the gang and told him we were being followed by four white men. I said they were not up to any good. We would stop for midday and pick a place where we would be well seen. Told them would again try to see what they were up to. Knew they would stay back just out of sight. Again found them dismounted and talking and not being very quiet about it, my dog gave a very light growl, just touched him and he stopped. They were planning on hitting us when we were camped that

3

night. They would have to come in from behind and the other two in from the other side. They had done this before could tell about how they were talking. Their comments were will have some fun with a woman before we scalp them. I then moved back to our midday camp, telling all about their plans.

We will ride until we find a spot where we can defend ourselves. Found a good spot just before dark. Then told how we would set up our ambush. I then told the girls not to hesitate to shoot if they did these men would kill at any of our mistakes. We set out our sleeping blankets and move them away from the fire. Told Guy and the girls not to look at the fire. This was to make sure their eyes would be used to the dark. Put Guy up to one side with Bess, Jan and Sue on the other, I would be watching for the others to come the other way. The fire had died down, my dog gave his warning and was then quiet. Watched as one man came my way. My arrow found its way to his chest he went down with a grunt. Guy and Bess fired about the same time. My dog attacked the other man, heard another shot Jan had fired. Could hear and see the other man fighting my dog couldn't get a clean shot at him for fear of hitting my dog. Call my dog off when the man stood up just put an arrow into him and Guy had reloaded and shot at the same time. Sue had held her shot just in case someone missed. She would be ready. The man Jan had shot was gut wounded. Sue was watching him he sat up and reached for his rifle, Sue said if he touched that he would another bullet coming. He then just sat there groaning he recognized a woman's voice. His next comment was, I was killed by a woman his curses then weren't pleasant to hear.

We were up the rest of the night my dog checking everyone then went and worried all the dead man just to be satisfied they were not a threat anymore. The man that was gut shot died lasted only another half hour, he just mumbled he knew he was going to hell. The next morning I and Guy search all of them they all had gold coin, we took all that was worth anything. One had a fancy tomahawk took that also. The girls

4

said it would be quite a chore to bury all four. My answer was they are going to be turned face down and left. No one argued, Sue nodded her head in agreement. Jan and Bess still were wondering how I knew they were following us. Told them the Indians had instilled this in me, how it worked didn't really know. Gonacheaw was much better at it than. Told them was glad it wasn't Indians they usual weren't that stupid. Also new at times they also were. Turned all the dead man over face down before leaving, Sue asked why. Indians believe the spirit would not be unable to follow by going into the earth. We left after I went and collected their horses and gear. By the looks they were traveling light. They must have been watching us at the trading Post and decided we would be an easy kill. To them the girls probably look like novices. I was sure glad the girls could all shoot well. Sue and her composure of holding back just in case. Was something commended her for. If the other had gotten his rifle one of us might not be here. Sue said well everyone else got to put a bullet into those bad guys. I offered to take her back and let her shoot one of them. This broke the tension and everyone laughed including Sue.

Knew everyone would love the Black Hills. Took our time and made camp early each day so we could enjoy our surroundings. A couple more days and found the old village place. Everything had grown up, this is where I was taken and then escaped and was adopted into the clan. We decided to keep going it would just midday. Told how the clan moved the village every so often. The new location was because the gardens would be more productive. The game more plentiful. We talked about Indian life. The men did the hunting, the woman did all the gathering of herbs berries and all the planning of corn and squash and other edibles. Had to tell about my raising heck with the woman when they went out berry picking. How running deer threatened me with a stick because I was stealing berries out of her basket. Would run behind my Indian mother for protection. How the others would laugh at my antics. There man would never think of doing what I did. My Indian brother would just stand guard.

Thankful that he did he save my hide that time. We came to another village site it had not been used in some time either. Continued on our trek, was getting a little apprehensive that we hadn't ran into any occupied village as yet. Knew they always had their gardens planted by now. So we moved on and found another village abandon. Stayed a day or two before moving on we started out early, my dog gave us a warning. This is when I had a Guy and the girls get the rifles out. My dog went ahead of me, I could now sense it was a bear not too far away. Made a cautious approach, a grizzly was feeding on a carcass. Went back to let everyone know what it was, they all wanted to see the bear. We approached into the wind, led them to a rise and motioned to be very quiet and move slow no noise. We were able to watch the bear for a while. He quit feeding and all of a sudden his nose went up in the air, cross breeze may have given him a whiff of our scent. Had everyone back off and head for the horses.

I was going to watch the bear and make sure he wasn't interested in us. The bear just walked around the carcass a few times he then went and laid not too far away. Knew now it was safe to leave. This was the first time they all had seen a grizzly. All had seen drawings but first one for real. The bear was a good size, told everyone they were hard to kill. They asked if I had killed any. Yes had killed a few but hunted them with a lot of caution not all alone always with others. Told them about the time the old grizzly had found us following him and he had made a loop to follow us. My tracker friend Gonacheaw knew right away what the bear was up to. He had most likely ambushed his ambushers before.

Then told how we all urinated in one spot to draw his attention. This is when we got four arrows into him. He raised heck for a few minutes then went down. All arrows had found their mark to the heart and to the lungs.

I told the gang how Gonacheaw could track anything. Man or beast couldn't outfox him. He would still laugh and say I was the only one he could not track. He was like chum and I brothers.

We had killed a deer and had a good meal. Then cooked up the rest of the meat this would last us a week or more. I was killing grouse with my bow. They couldn't believe I had shot one out of the air with a bow while riding my horse. A lot of practice and a good feel made it an ideal weapon, liked it because it was so quiet. We stopped at a different stream to bathe and do our laundry, was a welcome stop we weren't in a hurry I couldn't get over we weren't seeing any Indians or sign as yet. The next village spot was also barren. Wasn't going to take them to the sacred Lake, change my mind. Just hope that it would be all right to bring my family there. Would ask if we were approached. We got to the lake and no one was around. Couldn't find any recent sign of the old shaman. Found his old fireplace it had not been used in some time we unpacked set up our camp plan on staying for a few days or more. A couple of days went by, we all enjoyed swimming and a lot of splashing. I couldn't understand no one being around. This had been well guarded when I was here before. The old shaman had given Running Deer and I an any time welcome. We had used it a lot, didn't tell them about my experience with the old shaman. Still felt the pain from remembering. Hard for me to believe how happy I was again. Next day told Jan and the crew was going to make a scouting to see if there was any sign of Indians. Jan asked if she could go with me, I was more than glad to have her come along I then had Bess Guy and Sue set up our camp in a new location. Moving downstream away from the lake. At one time the lake was only on invitation. Didn't want to have a party of Indians find us without the invite. We we now had 14 horses, to watch. When we stopped we had to hobble the strangers to make sure they didn't roam where we had to hunt for them. Could tell they were used to being hobbled. Jan and I had found Indian sign but still not fresh. A couple of weeks old, I was not sure what to do and was about to turn back when Jan and I spotted three or four horses and men. We went forward with caution, I then recognize them from the clan that had given Running Deer and I a welcome on our honeymoon. Called out to them and they recognize me right away. They had thought I was dead, I introduce them to Jan. They were glad I had found another wife after losing Running Deer. Then we chatted for a while, then asked where the Chief and Gonacheaw were. They said they were now chasing Buffalo on the prairies. They were now on their way to the lake. The old shaman had died and asked to be left at the lake he loved. They said it was fitting I should be here for the ceremony he had directed them to perform. Told him I had other family with me could they also join. Their answer was Brave Hawk your family is our family. Had to close my eyes for a few seconds it hit me so strong. I looked up they were looking away and respect for my feelings. Then they all gave me a wallop and laughed. Jan was startled when they did this she didn't know what had just happened. At first she thought they were attacking me. I explained what they had said when I asked if all my family could join in the ceremony. When they told me all my family is also there's. Told Jan I had to collect myself by closing my eyes. This is when they looked away to let me get my composure back. We then headed back to the lake. Then went back and got Guy Bess and Sue introduced them to my extended family. Told them the old shaman who had loved this lake had died. He had instructed the Braves in a ceremony and to leave him at the lake. They would build a type of elevated cover for his body. It was encased in a leather and tightly bound. We all help to set up the site. Set up on poles overlooking the lake. Once this was made the body was also tied to the crossings. That evening the ceremony got underway. A fire was built under the body, the body was high enough not to be affected by the fire. Then one of the Braves sat in to fan powder into the flames, the other three started the dance, had to join in the ceremony. Jan Bess Sue and Guy just watched this went on until the fire died down. Then the chanting began and lasted for some time. Woke up the next morning laying on the ground with the other Braves, Jan came and covered me. Was going to apologize, Jan said no, that was a beautiful ceremony and we were very fortunate to be part of it. Felt a lot better then, found I and the others were famished.

Sue and Bess had already got the meal going. We then got to visiting, telling about where we had been and what I had been doing. The girls then said tell him about seeing the grizzly. When I told him this they got excited and wanted to go and get this bear. I proceeded to tell them it was a day's ride back to where we had seen it. Told them time didn't seem to matter to the Indians in the way it did to us. They then said they would help with the horses. When they looked at the extra horses we had gotten from the dead men, they then said Brave Hawk the men no longer ride their horses. Then told him it was true they no longer rode their horses. They all nodded and commented it was good, not good men. Guy and the rest want to know what were talking about. They recognize the horses the men rode and said they no longer rode their horses, I had agreed. They had told me good, they weren't good men. We all turned back and went to see if the grizzly was still there.

Another day's ride we stopped for the evening meal. The Braves asked if Jan was my new wife. I then added Guy Bess and Sue were also family. They were fascinated by the girls hair color. Then commented how fortunate to have so many pretty woman around, and they got a big laugh at the comment, acknowledge I was very fortunate. They then made a comment all the woman wanted to take care me and had another big laugh over this comment. Just kind of gave a grin and rolled my eyes. This brought on another gale of laughter. Jan Guy Bess and Sue knew they were ribbing me but didn't know what was being said had to translate. They also got a big kick out of what they had said. We had stopped a ways from where we had last seen the bear. Next morning had a quick meal. Then headed for where the bear had been feeding on a fresh carcass. Guy Bess Jan and Sue wanted to also be included. I decided to stay up on the ridge knowing the carcass was in the lower part of a small valley. The others went around to the other side could see them occasionally. My dog gave us a warning, I then knew the bear was somewhere close. The bear came out of concealment and attacked the brave just below us. I let an arrow loose and the brave shot with a rifle he was carrying. The bear was on him knocking him down. I pulled my knife ran and jumped on the Bears back and plunged my knife into his neck he made a swipe at me I again plugged my knife into his neck must have hit his spine because he just went flat without any more movement. Jan and Sue Guy and Bess had also ran down with me but didn't dare shoot for fear of hitting me or the brave under the bear. The Brave squirmed his way out from under the bear. He wasn't hurt except for a few bruises, he had used his rifle to protect himself and showed a lot of teeth marks on it. The other Braves had came on the run, but was all over when they got there. Jan's comment when she see I was okay just torn britches where he had swipe at me. I now understand why they call you Brave Hawk and proceeded to give me a hang on hug.

The Braves then skinned and gutted the bear. He was an older bear the hide would be used for moccasins it was kind of shaggy. The brave that was under the bear, told everyone he was glad I was his brother. It wasn't there custom to acknowledge thanks in a direct way. His just saying this made me feel good. Knew they would have a story to tell when we got back to the tribe. The other Braves were laughing at what had happened. Especially he being under the bear still coming out on harmed. Guy Bess Sue and Jan said they didn't know what to do everything happened so fast. They couldn't believe I had actually jumped on the Bears back. Took a few more days to prepare the meat for traveling. There wasn't a lot of fat on this bear. The Braves said he didn't seem to have as much fat as he should have. The fat was very important for their use, mixed it in a lot of their food.

Told our crew we were having a lot more problems than had not counted on. Thankfully we all came out unharmed. The whole bunch said this was the important part and they would have a tale to tell, that a lot wouldn't believe. Sue came over and gave me a hug saying she was so glad she had came along and don't fret about things they are turning out just fine. Jan Bess and Sue were keeping a log on our travels. The time was going by, we didn't realize how much time had went by. The Braves said it would be a half moon to where the clan was. They had joined together with my clan. the Indians were pleased that my mare was doing so well. They had to check out the two colts she had given birth to. We all offered them each one of the horses we had taken from the dead men. They refuse saying they had nothing to trade. I then told them they were giving us their know-how and guidance. We would never been able to find our family without them. They at first didn't know what to make of this. Enough insistence from us and they finally accepted.

They asked that evening if this is one of the white man's ways. Had to explain that doing something for another or others was how we sometimes would trade. Friends would give gifts without expecting anything in return. They didn't know if it was a good thing or a bad thing. They then asked me if I expected to be paid for saving the Braves life. My answer was a very strong no. Then explained we were brothers and that was all that was expected. They then asked about the white men we had done in. I told them most were very good men and woman. We like the Indians had a quite a few that were not good. They just took to help themselves even if it meant killing.

We were now on the plains and hadn't seen any Buffalo as yet. They then told us we were getting close could see sign. I also could see Buffalo sign with horses sign every so often. We could at times see for a very long distance. One of the Braves came back and pointed we could make out tepees in the distance told the crew were getting close now, the weather had been really hot. Thanks to the wind always seem to blow it helped keep us cool. As we neared we could see a lot of commotion. They had seen us coming, seemed like all came out to greet us. My adopted mother had age a lot more than I expected. She was ecstatic about seeing me still alive. She had to put her hands on my shoulders and turned me around to make sure I was all there. Everyone was then welcomed. My impression was that woman were having a lot harder time than when they were at the villages. Talk with them and they said they now just follow the Buffalo, this is their food source now. They had not planted any garden in quite a while. They never complain but could tell they missed the village life. Wouldn't be long and they would be moving again. They also knew where all the water sources were. Felt bad for them they weren't able to bathe until they had a river or good water source. Hadn't seen the Chief, Gonacheaw or little arrow. No more than got the words out when they came riding into the camp. Buffalo were not too far away, Chief and others got together to plan a hunt. My brother little arrow was also surprised to see me. We both stood with our hands on each others shoulders. He had really filled out, he was one solid Indian now. I told him I was not going to wrestle with them anymore. He then just laughed and said my childhood is over.

Next day the hunt was organized. Quite a few had acquired rifles. My brother Gonacheaw still used his bow. Asked if I could join them they said they expected me to. All rode horses now. They would still dismount and run alongside it to keep themselves in shape. I had always done this so this hadn't changed. Found the herd about midday. Road up behind slowly,.Jan Bess Sue and Guy had came with us just to see the hunt. They stayed back when I told them we were in the process of moving up to the herd. Decided to give chase would kill just one. The herd had been hunted before so they began to move. We then moved in before they got any momentum up, we all would pick out one and proceeded to try either get an arrow or a shot off. Rode up beside a young cow and got my arrow off and then backed off. Turn to see a big bull charging one of the Braves, tried to yell a warning but all the noise and commotion he couldn't hear me. He was concentrating on getting a shot off when the big bull hit him and his horse. They went tumbling then the big bull just followed the herd. I got there after one of the others got there. The brave had went over with his horse and they had both went down. He was one of the younger boys and didn't have the experience of the others. The horse was also badly injured, the boy it appeared had broken his neck in the tumble. This was going to be one sad hunt. Still had to take care of the downed Buffalo. The woman had packed up and weren't far behind.

The Braves mother was summoned and she keened for her son for quite some time. Jan Sue Bess and Guy had seen it happen. They told me later they didn't realize how dangerous it could be. The buffalo were massive animals. They wanted to know if there was anything they could do. I just didn't know myself. Told them would ask Gonacheaw what we could or should do. Gonacheaw answer was, we will have a ceremony to celebrate his life he was quite young and not as an experienced as most of the other hunters. We had six Buffalo down and the woman were already taking care of them. Once the buffalo were taking care of, a seven-day burial ceremony was started. The shaman was very old now but was still quite capable of doing all the ceremony. He told me he knew I was coming with my family, also the Chief new both were psychic and spiritually gifted.

This wasn't a very happy time for the tribe. My new family were welcome into the ceremony. The shaman and Chief insisted I was to be part of the ceremony. The boys mother also welcomed me and family. We would just sit with her and the others in helping her with her pain and sorrow. Joined the shaman and the Chief Gonacheaw and Little Arrow in this main ceremony. The Chief made the decision to move to a known water source to replenish and give all a welcome break. Found a new way of life was a lot harder on the woman. The older woman missed the attending of their gardens and of the semi-permanent villages they had established every few years to let the ground recover from planting. The shaman always knew when to move.

We established the camp near a river giving everyone a very nice break from the heat and dryness of the planes. Jan Bess Sue and Guy were at first stunned that the woman all went into the water naked. Had a good laugh at their expense. Told them this was a normal procedure, they still said they weren't going to join. We all set up camp a short distance then road up river to find a more secluded spot to do our bathing. We all welcomed the wet relief. We all decided to head back home in a few days, we informed the Chief and the shaman said he would have a ceremony for our safe journey. We were having a meal with everyone talking and telling of one, experience or an other some quite comical.

Five strange Indians road into the camp. They acted as though if they owned the place. Could see Chief and Gonacheaw quite upset. One we could tell was their leader. He kept eyeing Jan Bess and Sue. He finally asked who the woman belong to. Little arrow pointed at me, then he told him he wanted to trade for my woman. I knew what he was saying but didn't let on I could understand. Told little arrow to tell him that the woman had traded for me and I belong to them. This was supposed to be a joke. The others all laughed at this comment. He got very upset and then stood up, and said to little arrow and Gonacheaw that he would kill me and take my woman. I was on my feet and had my knife out and had it at his throat. I could see the flash of fear in his eyes, I then told him I just gave you your life leave now. The men that had heard him were on their feet as his four men were also up they just backed out of the camp with one kind of strutting. After they left I said I was going to have to watch on the way back home. He would give me trouble. We all sat back down to finish the meal, the meal had become very somber after that episode.

Our tents weren't that far from the village I also knew my dog and horse would give us warning. We had planned on leaving that the next morning. You, Shaman said sit for a while. Knew he didn't want us to leave until Chief and the other Braves got back. I then knew that they were out to take care of the insult the ones that had barge into the camp and openly threatened one of their own. About mid afternoon, Chief Gonacheaw Little Arrow and the others came back into camp. Gonacheaw with a big grin showed me the fancy tomahawk the strutted Indian had carried. He then stated we would have no trouble his spirit was face down with two others. This relieved me of the worry of trying to keep an eye out for him. We were now ready to leave, and saying our goodbyes all the girls and woman had to come and touch Jan and Bess's hair blondes and redheads had not been seen by most of the tribe. Gonacheaw Little Arrow would ride with us for two days to scout to make sure the two that had gotten away were not following us. We also thanked the Braves that brought us to our family. My Indian mother said she wouldn't be here when I came again saying the spirits would be watching over me.

The first day went off without any problems, the second day in the afternoon we could smell a terrible order. We came over arise and there was at least 100 or more Buffalo carcass rotting. Both my brothers were disgusted they all had been skinned and the meat was left to rot. The Indians couldn't understand how they could leave all that meat to spoil. At our trading post we had traded with just the Indians but never had had 100 hides at one time. 8 to 10 at times sometimes up to 20. With the Indians the meat never went to waste. I was going to try to stop this kind of slaughter There was enough buffalo to feed everyone. Why destroy an excellent food supply. We had a meal then parted, told him would try to get back a little sooner. They agreed and turned back.

It was a melancholy few days for me. Every thing went well for another few days, we made camp early in an afternoon to give me a chance to hunt grouse for supper. Made a change from the Buffalo meal and dried venison we have been eating. Jan said she would like to take a long run, she said it was needed to get her life back in shape from so much riding. I took off with her when I found good grouse cover let Jan know she should head back I would be back with grouse I hoped. Jan headed back to camp, luckily I got to grouse just shortly after leaving Jan. Thought I would be able to catch up with her. This is when I could hear horses, five or six men rode Jan down and one pulled her up onto his horse and kept on going. Knew would not be able to catch up on foot headed for camp let the others know what had just happened. Set them up so they could protect themselves, told them was going to get Jan back. Guy wanted to come with me. I told him it best that he stay and help protect the camp with the girls he reluctantly agreed. The trail wasn't very hard to follow. They were the buffalo hunters that had killed all the Buffalo. Rode quite hard at first, when they had slowed to a walk I did the same came on their camp just at dusk. They didn't seem to have any guards out.

Spotted Jan with one of the hunters he seemed to claim her as his. I just waited for a good opportunity, then rode my horse straight into the camp. The man next to Jan's step to stop me and I just ran him over. Leaning over with my arm out Jan grabbed hold and swung up on the back of my pony with me. Made a circle and headed back to our own camp Jan hanging onto me very tight when we got back they hadn't built a fire just in case I was gone all night. We got off my pony and got some very welcoming hugs, then told them I was going back to drive off their horses. They tried to talk me out of going. I then explained if I didn't they would probably give us a lot of trouble. They had rifles that could shoot from a long distance. After this episode they may just try something. Took my time and came up to the camp. Most were drinking they had posted one man is a guard. He was not very attentive, in fact he was sleeping quite soundly. The horses were all hobbled and not too far from their camp. Walked my mare and my dog into their mix and on hobbled them, then took the hobbles and snuck into the camp and laid the hobbles next to the sleeping guard. Then slowly moved the horses away with help of my dog kept them going to our camp. When I showed up they were primed and ready they weren't sure if it was me or the buffalo hunters. My dog keep the horses corralled. Told the crew were leaving. They had not on packed was in no time were on our way. We now had more horses than we knew what to do with. We just kept them heading ahead of us. Morning came and all agreed we should keep moving. We rode steady all day nightfall we then made camp.

We decided to scatter the horses that I had rounded up. Would next day run one or two out then keep moving they were capable of fending for themselves. We now rode more at a leisurely pace. Even though I knew most of the time when we were being followed I still checked on our back trail to make sure. Every so often we would run one or two with a horses off to let them fend for themselves. Some would come back and follow us. I knew there would be some very unhappy buffalo hunters. They wouldn't be able to move their buffalo hides. Was quite shore had round up all the horses, be a while before they would be able to get more. One heck of a long walk for them which was good. This sure didn't hurt our feelings any, just thinking about it made me laugh. I believe if I didn't have my family to look after, would have done them all in. I would've picked them off one at a time. When I told Jan what I had been thinking, she's was just glad I was able to get her out of that bunch. They were very rough bunch. Jan said the one who caught her was out voted by the others she would be shared by all

We now were getting close to the lake I loved. Then asked if they were willing to stop for a while have a good meal and enjoy the lake. We packed up again all were anxious to get back to the post especially the girls. We then headed back to the trading post, less than a week's ride and we were there. Chum was also there to greet us. He said he had calculated about when we would be back. He had been there for more than two weeks. Chum and Sue had a wonderful reunion with a party. Chum had brought wine with him and kept it cooled in the stream, the men at the post joined in with us. We all had a good time, later I asked about the four men who had followed us. Our men said they had stopped and wanted some whiskey. They became quite belligerent when none was forthcoming Judd our man in charge had his two men poked their rifles out at them. Jan had overheard me asking about them. He also said they had posted one of the men as a guard to watch out for them, he was sure they would be back to try to rob them. Jan spoke up and said you don't have to worry about them anymore they're all dead. They were surprised to hear this they wanted to know what it happened. Judd then motioned for his men to come and listen to what Jan had to tell about the four men. Chum hadn't heard about it either, so he joined in. Jan was a very good storyteller she described every detail of what had happened. Chum spoke up after and said he now was sorry he had not come with us. He was sure glad that everyone came out okay. I knew he would ask Sue if Jan had embellish the story. Sue's answer was no she's left some of it out and they laughed at Chum. He just gave Sue a fierce hug. He told Sue he had gotten back to the farm and in a few days was sorry he had not came along. He knew we were more than a week out and decided not to try and follow us. Sue then gave him a big hug.

We were all anxious now to get back to the farm. Not too many days and we rolled into the farm. Mom and Chuck was there to greet us. We all had a wonderful welcome, family and friends including our cook and maids. They all wanted to hear about our travels and experiences. The stories were hard for some to believe. We told everyone how good it was to be back on the farm.

Had to go to the sawmill just to see how well the improvements had worked out. Chum said he missed me very much not just for friendship but because I seem to know how to set things up and how to work out the problems. He said he had a hard time of it and was sure glad I was back. The mill was running quite well but the plainer was always giving a problem. I said between the two of us we should be able to figure things out. Would like to go into the city and check out their system again. They were setting up a steam engine, maybe we could do the same here.

Jan Bess and Guy were anxious to go back to the city. They knew their friends would be glad to see them also will want to know about their travels. Chuck told us that he mom and Chum were worried in the last couple of weeks, thought we should have been back weeks before. I know they didn't realize it how far we actually traveled. Hadn't planned a trip out on the planes. It was hard for me to visualize how the horses had change I

Indians lifestyle and just of very few years. Some Indians had horses longer than my Indian family. When I told mom how far we had gone she then understood why were late in getting back. Our next plans were to get set to go back to the city. At first mom wasn't going to go. Chuck then stepped in and said now Mary we had a wonderful time when we were in the city the last time. Chuck said I'm definitely going and love to have you with me. Mom just grinned and then agreed this made me feel quite good to see mom and Chuck getting on so well Chuck had to grin and give mom a big hug. All of our traveling everyone had learned to travel light. No extras just bare necessities. Wasn't much for Jan Bess and Guy to be ready to leave. We stayed at the farm for a couple of weeks to settle down and relate more of our traveling experiences.

The farm was doing very well, we had good help, Chuck had hired a working foreman who did a good job of keeping things organized. He wasn't hard to work for, he was reasonable but firm. All the help like him because of his fairness. Chuck told me he was one of his close friends from the time of his carefree days in the city. Both mules had died first one then that shortly the other followed I did miss seeing them. They had been a big part of my early life. Jan and I roamed the farm and also spent time at our private lake and cabin Chuck and Chum had made many improvements on the cabin now more like a house with bedrooms. Also had glass windows overlooking the lake. With our sawmill we had ready access to all the lumber we needed. This was a wonderful place for relaxing and enjoying nature. Sue and Chum spent over a week at the lake, they said it was there second honeymoon.

Everyone is ready for the city. We were soon packed up and on our way. Chuck had one of the men bring a two wheel cart for our supplies and overnight stays Chuck had just come back with supplies and wasn't going to bother with wagons this time. We're going more for shopping and enjoyment. Mom has seen Jan and Bess not riding sidesaddle anymore. She decided to do the same and found it much more comfortable plus easier to control her mare. Our travel was very pleasant, took our time stopping often for tea and early evening for supper. When we got to the city Jan insisted we stay with her father. He would more than welcome us also had plenty of room for everyone.

On the way the road was getting quite rough. Some of the streams were getting deep ruts from heavy wagons. If one got stuck they were on their own or had to wait for some help to get pulled out. Chuck said he was always prepared and had an extra team that used to switch to give the other team rest. When he did get stuck the second team was always this extra power they needed to get pulled out. Very seldom do they have to unload to get unstuck. We had repaired the lower part of the road ourselves. One evening at supper Chuck asked Chum and I are thoughts about making a toll road on the part we kept repairing. Chum and I thought it a great idea. We had to acquire the rights to the roadway at least for the part we had repaired. Sue and mom commented this would be a big undertaking. We had a lot going on on of the farm and the sawmill. Chuck then said we would hire the help to do all the work and would have a foreman see to the men we hired they would have to have their own horses we could furnish the carts to haul the gravel. We could also build the bridges to cross the streams, we had the sawmill to cut the timbers for planking. Would have to set up toll gates at each end. Had come up with all to charge the in between people as yet. We knew our true toll gates would have to be at most bridges. Anyone traveling with a wagon would have a hard time fording most streams. A lot of planning would have to go into the project.

When we went to Jan's father's house we were welcomed with open arms. Chum and Chuck had a lot of friends and business acquaintances. Most knew about Jan Bess Guy in our travels Jan's father Henry couldn't wait to hear about our exploits and all the traveling we did. When Jan told him we were out on the planes with the Indians, his comment was he had thought we were only going to meet my Indian family. Jan said they had moved on to the planes to hunt buffalo. Dad you won't believe all experiences we had and thank goodness for bird he knew how to handle every challenge

All Henry's help was treated like family, they all came to see us. Henry's cook was like an old mother hen she knew how to organize the household. The large dining room had a very large table also. To help all gathered for supper and food was passed very informally. The maids had to serve only when Henry had a big party. They had a hard time waiting for everyone to finish eating so they could hear about our exploits. Jan and Bess were very good at relating are traveling experiences everyone was enthralled when Jan and Bess told about our first week out how we had done in four men who had planned on doing us in. Seemed all had questions of how this came about. Just as part of our travels took up the main evening. Henry told me after the meal and we were having a glass of wine, bird you are a dang Indian and we all laughed at his comment Guy also got a big kick out of this. Henry said thank goodness you had the experience or none of you would've been here to tell about it.

Chuck brought up the subject of a toll road that we had talked about on the way to the city. Henry told us he knew about toll roads. He said he didn't recommend doing this. He then explained that he had been involved with a toll road, it was one headache after another. You got your road and bridges in good shape the wagoneers started to overload their wagons. The bridges wouldn't stand up to the extra heavy loads and the roads also became very rutted with just a few overloads. It was a constant hassle. You also had to have trusted men collecting the tolls. Henry also said there were many other problems that would come up. He said he sold his share and made a small profit but was glad to get out of it. Chuck Chum and I changed our minds about a toll road immediately. We didn't need all the hassle. Mom Sue and Jan were also glad we decided not to choose this endeavor. The farm and the sawmill were doing very well. Also Chuck and retained some rights in this blacksmith shop so we also came first when we had to have something done. We would use the equipment ourselves at times, other times he would have the two blacksmiths and their help do the work for us. We always paid them even though they didn't want to charge us.

Chuck Chum and I were anxious to go to the city blacksmith shop to see how the steam engines had worked out. Waited until after the party that Henry had planned. He hired extra help to take a load off his own people. Henry's foreman took over the outside and the care of the horses and carriages his head cook organize all the inside work and he told her she was a fussy one made sure everyone was doing their jobs. Guy suggested we all go up to his cabin for the day. Mom and Chuck had other plans Chum Sue Bess Guy Jan and I decided to go just to see how things had changed. This is also a nice spot on a small lake. Guys father had work done on the cabin. He also had an out cabin for the caretakers. The ride out was pleasant enjoying the fall foliage. We had brought our own food and drink we had a good spread enjoyed our meal. The care taker was very belligerent. Guy decided to have a talk with them. It looked as though he had been using the main cabin for some of his own partying. I Told Guy to be very careful didn't like the way he was acting. Guy decided he was going to fire him, hadn't brought my bow but my small rifle was always with me on my mare. Went and got it and just in case the caretaker would cause a problem. Guy told him he had been using the cabin for partying. He tried to deny this but the evidence of the empty bottles in the cabin being filthy was something you couldn't ignore. Next guy told him to pack up and leave now. He went back to the cabin he was supposed to use when he came out he had his rifle. I was watching from the side and hollered at Guy to duck into the woods he raised his rifle to fire at Guy this is when I hollered at him, he spun and we fired at at the same time, his shot was off while my shot was to the heart wasn't about to let him get away with trying to kill one of us the girls and Chum were still down at the lake where we had had our meal Chum came on the run dodging from tree to tree just in case the caretakers had shot at us Guy hollered it was okay. Chum came up then and wanted to know what had happened Guy said the caretaker had tried to shoot him. Bird was shot at and then return fire and did the caretaker in. We hollered for the girls they came up to the lake then Guy told the girls and Chum, how Bird senses how these persons are going to act I wish I knew. The next question would we call in the sheriff. My answer was no we will bury him over in the swamp face down. Guy would tell his father. We all should just forget that it happened would have to hire another caretaker hoping has a woman this time. Everyone was quite sober on the way back to the city. When we arrived Guy asked me if I would accompany him when we told what had happened. Guys father was upset but was glad everyone was okay he then said he would tell the sheriff. They were very good friends. This way any inquires about him the sheriff would handle. We would meet the sheriff at Henry's party. The party was a great success Jan and Bess were bells of the evening after the meal Jan and Bess narrated about our travel and experiences some thought they were embellishing on our stories. They had even left out some of the details then and Sue would inject some of the details also. Poor mom just shook her head and commented how you all live threw this is amazing. The first part of us doing in the four men that attacked us was hard for some to believe.

Henry met with the sheriff and he told Henry that he was sure Bess's father had hired the wrong man. He said he just forgot about it he also warned us about another man who didn't like Chuck or Chum. He was commenting that Chuck and Chum had outbid him on some of his doing. And he wasn't happy about this. The sheriff said to watch our step he was very vindictive. Even though he had been wrong, just took a dislike to us. Bess's father had sent workmen and woman to clean the cabin and repair any of the damage done by the last caretakers one man and his wife would be the next new caretakers. They were recommended by the sheriff very knowledgeable about the criminal activity also a real good judge of people. A few days after the party Jan Bess guy went to take a ride out to their cabin to see the progress.

Mom Sue Chuck and Chum had other plans some included business. I definitely wasn't the businessman Chuck and Chum had become. They were always treated well because of their honesty. They would dicker on prices were always fair and all their dealings Jan Bess packed our lunch and we were off. My filly was beginning to show her age. Still in real good shape by slowing down some. I would run along side of my filly rather than ride all the time. Jan even started doing the same. I had learned this from my Indian brothers could run a good trot all day. Jan was also doing real well. Bess and Guy would remark how in the world I did this was beyond them.

When we arrived at the cabin their were still men working there, the new caretakers were there also helping out. Everything was going well, one more day would finish up. We had a good rapore with the workers and new caretakers being new they didn't have much to say. Just answered our questions as best they could. Jan and Bess said they treated us like royalty. The girls knew that the workers would still be there, had packed plenty for all to share. At first they were reluctant to join us, with Jan and Bess's insistence they finally agreed. We had a real nice time. When they realized we weren't trying to put ourselves above them, they relaxed and we all enjoyed the luncheon and the talking.

They had heard about our expedition and were anxious to hear some of our stories. Jan and Bess were more than glad to oblige I asked the workers if any odd characters had shown up. They had approached them to inquire about the other caretaker. They had told them he had been fired. They then told the workers he had told them he owned the place. Then informed them again that he had been fired and they he had left. Two of them laughed and commented he was a dang good liar. We'll just have to find another place to do our partying, they then left.

The workmen had done a lot of repair also brought new furniture replacing the smash pieces. Wouldn't be long and it would be quite comfortable again. We packed up and headed back to the city, I had had a good run so road along with everyone just bantering back and forth. Mentioned to Guy we were planning a trip to the blacksmith. They had installed a steam engine, Chuck Chum and I were very interested in finding how well it worked out for them. Told Guy about the policeman that had set me up against some knife wielding scum. And how I had survived. This had happened close to the blacksmith shop. They usually knew what was going on. After the second assault just a few days later the policeman was found in the river with his skull caved in. Told Guy this is the kind of friends you need. Guys answer was I already have them and I couldn't ask for better than you and your family. Didn't make a comment but it gave me a good feeling.

Living with the Indians had adopted the ways to some extent. Most would acknowledge this comment but Indians never did it was just a known. We that is Chuck Chum Guy and myself had talked about going to the blacksmith shop at the party. So it was common knowledge we would be going in a couple of days got together and we all decided to walk, it was a couple of miles. The shop was set up near the river and next to a stream for water power. The three owners were always looking for something new. They had purchased a steam engine. The steam engines were common further east. It had been some time since we had been to the blacksmith shop. We had sent word we were coming and wanted to take them out to dinner.

After breakfast with the girls going shopping we got ready for our trip to the blacksmith's. Mom never showed her excitement we knew she always enjoyed the forays. It was quite lively with the girls and aunt Sue. Mom would tried to shush them to no avail. She had made the comment how much she enjoyed these outings.

I decided to go to the stable to check out my dog and filly before going to the blacksmith to check out the steam engines. When arriving two of the men came out and told me that this man with two dogs had come by and had seen my dog lay outside of the stable where my filly was. He had sicked his two dogs on my dog, there was a hell of a fight my dog had killed both his. My dog was in real bad shape. They also told me the man said he would be back. He wasn't happy about my dog killing his.

Went back and got some help to see if Mom and Sue could do anything to help. Sue was packing him up when this man showed up. He then said who's dog is that. I stepped forward drew my knife and put it to his throat. I could see the fear in his eyes, he then said your dog killed my dog. My answer was I was about to kill him. Sue held my arm and I just backed down. He then thought it darn good idea to leave. We patched up my dog as best we could, the hostler's I trusted said that he would take care of my dog. I knew my dog would be a lot more comfortable near my filly and he also trusted the hostler.

We would be heading back to the farm before too long. Would keep him in one of the wagons he was tore up too much for them to travel on his own. Sue said you were ready to do that man in if I hadn't stepped in, and I admitted it was very close. Sue said you just made another enemy. The hostler said he had been here before looking things over. This is when he came back with the two dogs and sicked them on my dog. I was worried my dog might not survive. Told Chuck and chum what had happened at the stable. We then decided to walk to the blacksmith. Chuck and Chum lit up cigars Guy and I refrained. We didn't mind the smell but smoking was out of the question for us. Tried it once and it made me sick wasn't about to try again.

About a quarter of a mile or less from the shop six men with knives and clubs stepped out from the side street. Chuck said back into this doorway so we can protect our backs. I had already drawn my knife, Chuck and Chum and Guy had done the same. We were then waiting for their next move. All of a sudden one of the assailants went down with a hard grunt then another just seem to fall on his face. We were hard-pressed at first what was going on. The three blacksmiths had heard by their informants, kids mainly what was going on. They had each taken iron balls the size of a fist. They had started to peg at our attackers, one had been hit in the back another in the head the other four left in a hurry two limping as they left. The blacksmiths came to meet us laughing as they came, the one who had been hit in the back was trying to get up. One of the blacksmith just kicked him in the face and he went down again. These are some real rough man. We then asked them how they knew this was about to happen. Their answer was we have a bunch of informers we paid to keep us up all the things that are going on. Surprised us when they said all were really young boys they never seem to exaggerate just told him what they had heard..

They then went looking for the iron balls they had thrown. With our help gather up all we could find. I said that was quite a weapon. They said it was great if they weren't expecting it, if they were they could always duck some of the balls. They had also came prepared with their knives and cudgels. I still had my knife in my hand in one of the Smithy's asked how many I had done in with my knife. He then just guffawed. This was the knife they had made for me sometime before. Chuck said just kidding more than a few, this made them all laugh again.

We stopped in a pub for a beer at their insistence. Then headed for the shop. We found the steam engines were working out real well. They had to keep a good pile of wood on hand to feed the boilers. Sometime in the summer the stream would slow up enough so didn't have the power to run the mill. This is when the steam engine came into play. Even sometimes in the winter the stream would freeze up and they would use the steam engines than. Chuck Chum and I decided this would be a good investment. We had all kinds of wood to burn fuel would be no problem for us. Chuck and Chum would do all the negotiating for the engine. We weren't sure as yet for two smaller engines instead of one large one. One would run the main mill the other would run the shaper and plainer. New belts were being perfected all the time. Cotton and other fiber such as hemp were being used and tried for endurance.

Guys father Joseph planed another big party to celebrate our safe return from our Western travels. Bess's father not to be outdone had planed another party for our safe return. Mom laughed and said we would be partied out by the time we get back to the farm. At the party we knew someone there had set up for the attacked on us. Without our blacksmith friends the outcome may have been a lot different. One man was over friendly, Chuck said don't turn your back on him. Word from some others told us he was treacherous. We talked it over and decided not to confront him, we would keep our eyes open and rely on our blacksmith friends for information. They would send a couple of young boys to inform us. Told Joseph to expect a couple of ragamuffins, they were messengers for us. We would give them a good tip, the blacksmith did the same so they were paid twice. Wasn't long before they showed up with a note for us. Henry had received from the boys, our suspicions were true. The blacksmiths had threatened one of the men by sticking his head toward the forge, he immediately told who had hired him and the others. Henry said the sheriff has some good man who we could hire for us to keep track of his shenanigans. We agreed definitely needed all the help we could get.

Still we didn't know why he had it in for us, mom and the girls had not been told. We didn't want them to worry. The girls mom and Sue had finished all their shopping and were ready to go home. We were packing up and getting ready to leave when one of our men hired to watch over our adversary showed up. He then told us what he had observed. They had packed up and were well armed renting horses at one of the stable. They headed down the road we would be taking two back to the farm. We figured they were out to ambush us somewhere on the road. We had to tell mom Sue and Jan so they would also be prepared. Guy and Bess were staying in the city, Guy had to catch up on his and his father's business. His father had really missed him and Bess, looking forward to grandchildren.

We were on Our Way, Chuck and his two men would stay with the woman. Chum would stay back to watch the rear. I was to do the scouting out front. We traveled leisurely setting up watches all night. Everything seemed to be quiet. I hadn't detected anything out of the ordinary. I had the same feeling as my friend Gonacheaw, we just seem to know when someone was hiding to attacked us. So far had come across nothing, could make out the horses tracks. They had stopped to camp but had not so far set up an ambush. They were quite easy for me to track thanks to Gonacheaw. We were getting close to the end of our journey. I came back toward evening and told everyone had a bad feeling, they may have attacked the farm instead of trying to ambush us. We only had one more day's ride would everyone be willing to ride all night. Everyone agreed I would still stay out front to make sure of no ambush.

By morning were almost to the village, daylight we were passing through the village. The men had definitely attacked the farm. When we arrived everything was in turmoil. Chuck and chum were going to follow them through the woods. I told him I would follow on foot they would not be able to travel very fast and I could catch them told Chuck and Chum to take extra rifles and my mare and hurry up the road to the mainstream we had crossed. I was sure they would follow the stream to the main road. Chuck and Chum wasted no time in getting things together. I took off and trotted to the woods on their track. Sure enough they hit the stream and were following it. Could tell they weren't in a hurry. They wouldn't be expecting anyone to follow this soon. Wasn't long and had caught up to them. Decided to wait till they hit the road. They had stopped for a break, could hear them arguing some wanted to keep going. He said he would not feel safe till back in the city.

I knew now by this time Chuck and Chum were set up. so instead of starting my attack, would wait till they had hit the road. Wasn't more than an hour and they were at the road.. Put an arrow into one and knocked him off his horse, two others went down at almost the same time. The last one headed up the road on a gallop but another shot knocked him off his horse also. Three were dead the other was still alive. When we questioned him he had no idea who had hired them. Another man approached them, set them up with horses and guns and supplies. Were told it would be an easy raid the farm wasn't protected. He died shortly after the questions. We retrieved all their belongings and all they had taken. Our money was well hidden so they had not found it. I was just going to strip them and leave them face down. Chuck and Chum said they would either come back and bury them or have some from the village do it.

Chuck was the sheriff so he would write up a report just in case there were any questions about what had happened. I was all for going into the city and shooting the so-and-so. Chuck and Chum talked me

30

out of it. Chuck said there are other ways of getting to him without us being directly involved.

Getting back to the farm, mom Sue and Janet calmed everyone down. Our foreman had been clubbed but was coming around. The woman had been threatened with rape, then the leader told them that others had escaped and probably headed for the village so they had to get out now. They all then left through the woods. They didn't dare go back through the village, they had thought the villagers would be ready for them. If they had went to the village the villagers were not organized and some will just close the doors and hide. The blacksmiths and his men were the few that would have confronted them. Myself was glad they had taken the woods. Telling Chuck and chum of their bickering only one actually had any woods experience. He was the leader, the others were questioned him how he knew if this stream was the same one that crossed the road. His reply finally was go your way and I'll go mine. The bickering stopped and they all followed him. If they had split up things wouldn't have gone so well for us.

Chuck told mom Sue and Jan how everything had went. Mom and Sue and Jan let the rest of our farm help know what had happened and all four men were dead. They wouldn't have to worry about them coming back again. Chuck Chum and I checked out the horses. Chuck determined they were from a stable that rented out horses by the day or the week. Chuck Then Told Me He and Chum would take the horses back and find out who had paid for their hire. We may find out some more information to make sure of our suspicions. I had planned on going with them. Chuck said to me please Bird stay at the farm, the farm needs a leader right now. Chum and I will handle the city part, I knew they were a lot more city wise than I was. I agreed was not happy not being involved. Chuck said if you hadn't of told us to set up the ambush at the stream, some would probably would've gotten away. Your Indian knowledge really came through. The city is where we know how to go about things. Chum and I know if you came you would confront this man. We as yet just don't have the proof. He has many paid for friends that will lie for him so we'll proceed with caution. Told Chuck I know you're right. Bird I'm glad you're not hardheaded like a lot I run into in our trading. Also found they had tried to burn the house, when they had seen some of the help head for the village, the four pile stuff in a couple of corners and lit it on fire. All decided this is what they had come for and decided to make their escape before the villagers showed up. They had taken valuables that were obvious but found no money. They're traveling through the woods to encounter the stream had slowed them up. The woman and help had extinguishing the fires before they had a chance to do any damage. Smoke and odor was the only residue and scorch corners. We had running water in the house plus outside were water troughs for horses and the cows. Very little damage had occurred a lot of clean up.

Chuck Chum and I decided to procure two steam engine for our sawmill. This would also make a good cover for investigating who had sent the four men to raid and burn our home. Mom Sue and Jan and the help cleaned up the house and set everything back to normal. Mom and Sue had different herbs to offset the smoke smell. Mom decided to have a dinner for everyone including all the help, the help wanted to know if any of the raiders had gotten away. They knew I had followed their sign in to the woods and Chuck and chum had left in a hurry. Chuck told them what had happened and all four were dead he had also made a report and filed it at the village. He was our County Sheriff. Our foreman was recovering from the blow he had received to the head, one very large lump. The dinner went well with a lot of talking about their doings. We all knew that the quick action saved the house, they hadn't tried to burn any of the outbuildings when they had seen some of the help head for the village they left shortly, afraid help was on the way.

Chuck and Chum and the help and I got the large wagon ready for the trip to the city. Two of the help would manage the wagon. Mom was glad I was staying behind the foreman and I were the only two men some young boys at the farm. The woman always pitched in doing the chores. Taking my usual walk in the woods around the farm again felt uneasy spotted two men watching the house. This didn't sit right with me. Watching them for quite a while they finally left. They waited till almost dark came back to watch the house. Told mom Sue and Jan something didn't look right. They were watching a house for some reason. Told Sue and Jan to load their rifles and have them at easy reach just in case. I had a sense something was going to happen. Jan I went to our room but didn't go to bed. She could tell from my action I wasn't about to sleep. So we just sat and whispered back and forth not to keep others awake. And Sue knew about my premonitions, she wasn't about to sleep either. Jan and I were getting a little sleepy got to giggling trying to stay awake. We were thinking about going to bed when the main door latch made a noise. We were wide-awake immediately the door was barred, the next thing the door was kicked open I stood with my rifle on the ready, and Sue at her room door. She fired her rifle at the intruder he went staggered back out the door. We then heard his companion mount his horse and leave in a hurry. I went out the window to check out that no one else was about then the woman with their lamps when I gave the okay the big man was laying on his back with his pistol still in his hand. We checked them over recognize this is the bully of yesteryear was the one that I had beaten so badly. I told the girls would take care of him. Next morning would try to find the other man. Through a rope around the dead man and headed into the woods dragging him behind one of our work horses. Got a good ways into the woods flipped him on his face and left him.

When I got back to the house the two blacksmiths were there. They also had been watching these two men. When a couple of villagers said

33

they were sure they had headed for our farm, they saddle up and were on their way. When this man came racing toward them, they had blocked the road with their two horses forcing the other horse to veer sharply dumping him off. He went limping off into the woods. We came out to see if everyone was okay, the coffee was started to brew we all sat and talked about what had happened.. The blacksmith said he won't get very far everyone will be on the lookout for him. After relating what had happened and everyone was calmed down the blacksmiths left. We and our help to keyed up to go back to bed, almost time to get up anyway.

I was just getting ready to go out and track this other man down when one of the villagers showed up saying they had this man tied up at the blacksmith shop. later in the day Sue Jan and I went into the village to confront this man. The blacksmiths were waiting for us, I asked him why he was traveling with this man. He said he fell in with him about six months ago or so. They had robbed other places but waited till no one was home. This time they watch the house and all they had seen were just woman. His partner said it would be an easy touch and would have fun with the woman. He promised not to do anything like this again if he was let go. The villagers listened and all decided to hang him the next morning. It was up to the villagers, they all determined it could have been one of their families. He was hung the next morning with a lot of pleading and crying from him.

We weren't at the hanging had enough trauma for a long time. Six men dead in less then week. Asked Sue how she felt about shooting this man. She said I remember you telling me not to hesitate when we had been attacked by the men on our trip out west because they would not hesitate. She said she didn't feel bad knowing now what his intentions were. How the blacksmiths knew was one of the villagers had stepped out at his house to relieve him self when he saw the men head up our farm road. He then went to the blacksmiths to let them know. This is when they mounted up and were able to block the road. The villagers were now alert and had captured him.

I could hardly wait to get the new steam engines. Getting them set up was going to be a lot of enjoyment for me. Had been up to the mill for a while, checked everyone to make sure they were okay and settle back down, then headed for the mill. They were already running when I got there. Waited till noon break and got everyone together and told then we would be setting up steam engines. Would be quite a project. Would have more power also would be running two engines. One for the saw the other for the planner and the other tools some we had made and some we had bought.

Chuck and chum hired other wagons to haul the engines and boilers that we needed to make the steam. Had to have extra teams pulling the wagons. Slow going because of the weight almost a full month before they arrived at the farm. Everyone was curious all had to look over the equipment, the road to the sawmill was quite good from all the travel and the repair our men had done to it. Chuck told me nothing had broken down but had got mired in a few times, a lot of extra work getting out of the mud. The men at the mill were waiting for us and had timbers and rollers ready for unloading. Foundations had already been built for the boilers and engines. We would put buildings up after things were in place. The men that came with the equipment also were there to set up the boilers and help with the engines and piping. In less than a month we're up and running. Just had to work out the few kinks I also told our man that was was running the boiler to make sure he cleaned the safety valve every day, we did not need the boilers blowing up.

Sue had told Chum about our episode with her shooting the intruder. He was quite surprised, then said I should have known you have plenty of grit. Mom also had informed Chuck about the episode. It was hard for him to believe after killing four men that someone had tried to raid the house. Told him what the other man had told us about only seeing woman around the house and thought it would be an easy raid. Chuck Chum and I had gone into the villagers to thank them for their help and for hanging the other man. Word would get out this was a place not to try to raid. Chuck then told me he was glad I had stayed behind. How I had recognize there may be trouble, Bird he said it had to be your Indian side. I always seem to sense troubles of this kind and to react to such. The men at the mill were starting to settle into the new routine. Found the engines had more power than our waterwheel. This helped make the plainer run without stalling. We were glad we had made another road away from the main farm, it was getting quite a lot of traffic for the lumber we were putting out. Most of the villagers had wooden floors now. Our foreman kept tabs on all our sales. Lot of the villagers didn't have ready cash, so when they wanted lumber it was in trade for livestock pigs chickens and vegetables. We then carted them off in the city with a good profit. Ended up working out well for us and the villagers.

Soon found Jan and Bess were both pregnant, and Sue was hoping she would be also be but still nothing. A lot of planning by mom and Sue, the whole farm was excited. Our help had had babies but were still born or died shortly after birth mom and Sue fussed over Jan until she put her foot down and told them she was going to do everything until she wasn't able to. Mom and Sue got a big chuckle out of this. They realize that they were being overprotective. Bess had sent word to mom asking if she could come and stay to have her baby at the farm. We were all thrilled to have Bess put so much confidence in mom. She stated since our trip out West she was much more comfortable at the farm. The time seem to fly, next we had two babies one a little girl the other a little boy. My first was a little girl, Bess and Guys with the little boy. They were both doing great, Jan and Bess both had a normal birthing. I couldn't wait till they were old enough to to teach them about everything. Bess and guy talked things over with Chuck and mom asking if she could live with us. She said it was a lot better to raise a child on the farm than in the city. Mom and Chuck and the rest of us were more than happy to have her and the baby with us. We then planned on an extension on the house. Jan was thrilled to have her best friend stay with us, they were like sisters.

Chum and I were in our element when it came to building extension. A lot of planning and input from the rest of the family. We got started and wasn't very long everything was up. Chuck even brought a glass for the Windows from the city. Our big project now is naming the two babies. Bess and guy had already came up with a name for their boy, Chad was to be it. Jan and I were having a hard time with the name for our little girl. We tried many different names but just couldn't settle on any that seem to fit. Mom and Sue had suggested a few also. We just couldn't seem to hit the name we liked. Mom then told me your aunt Sue had a sister that had crossed over when she was quite young. Mom asked Sue if she thought it was appropriate to bring her name up. Sue agreed saying it would be wonderful if we decided on her name for our daughter. Her name was Laura Lee, Jan and I looked at each other and decided immediately that was to be our daughter's name. We couldn't wait to tell Bess we had finally found a name that was also in the family. Could see mom was happy we had chosen Sue's sister's name for our daughter. Jan and I loved the sound of it, to us it's rang like a musical bell. Wasn't long everyone settled in. Guy would make the trip from the city once a month and stay for two or three days sometimes a week. Guy was thrilled to see how well Bess and his little boy were doing, saying it was a good move to have Beth stay at the farm. My filly was slowing down was afraid she would be turned out to pasture before long. Started riding the Colts.. Both were as big as she I had them trained quite well they were used to my way of riding, still road without a saddle. Had let my filly out to pasture while riding the Colts. Couldn't call them Colts anymore they were fine horses. Still doing a lot of puttering at the mill getting the plainer to work better. We found had to step up the speed of the cutters. Had to make up oil cups keep the bearings lubricated. Rollers next to the blades kept the board from chattering and ruining them. We had an excellent group of men at the mill, a few were from the city all got along real well. A couple asked for a couple of weeks to go visit their family in the city. Our foreman came to Chum and me. Chum and I told our foreman to give them each a weeks pay and tell them we expect them back in two weeks. They were shocked had never heard of getting paid and not working. They promised to be back. The other men were surprised also. Chuck and I told him we would shut the mill down for the two weeks and all get a weeks pay. Our foreman couldn't get over this. We said we have good men and we want to keep them. The mill was doing real well, the customer would have to wait for their lumber. Our foreman then came back and said we would just shut the plainer down. The men had agreed to split up and one bunch would work one week, the other the next week. So the mill didn't get shut down entirely. Chum and I decided this was a good time to make up different cutters for the plainer. Some now wanted fancier molding. We drew up what we wanted and took them to the blacksmith shop. A lot of experimenting and finally got things working quite well. We found it would be much easier to change out the whole cutting head. We would not have to keep adjusting the blades. The next was to get cutting heads made. In the meantime Chuck had been working in the city to try to find out who had hired the men to raid our farm. Chuck told us he now knew who it was but didn't have any proof. The two men that had rented out the horses told Chuck who had rented them. Chuck started checking and found it was one of the this mans hired hands. The next thing that happened both these man came up missing we had planned on using them as witnesses. Even the books were destroyed when Chuck went back to the stable. We will catch up to him when he least expects it was Chuck's answer. We were still upset over why this man had planned this.

Even the Sheriff couldn't figure it out. We just told Chuck to be damn careful and not to travel alone. Our blacksmith friends had put the word out don't try anything with Chuck the penalty would be extreme. Between the blacksmiths and their informers in a good friend the Sheriff we were able to keep track of this man. He had made no attempt to start another raid he just knew the men he hired had never came back. Then he covered his dealings up by getting rid of the books and shutting the stable men up who had furnished the horses. We had no proof of his actual connection to this. The farm was doing quite well mom was very good with the books with Sue's help. Jan and Bess were keeping busy with the babies, both were doing really well. Both Jan and Bess didn't want to get pregnant again for some time. Mom and Sue had a tea she had told them to drink every morning. This was the same tea they used on our trip West. This had been passed down from her mother and from her grandmother also. Chum and I supervise the farm and are harvesting of goods to be shipped to the city. Also spent time at the mill it was running great. We had more customers than we could really handle. We didn't overcharge but are prophets were substantial. Chum and I made sure the farm crops were rotated every season. Squash beets potatoes carrots pumpkins were our main ones. A lot of call for them and they didn't spoil easily. Our goods in the city were bought up and then redistributed by others. We found all of a sudden some of our buyers were willing to pay our prices, our prices had been very reasonable. Chuck found a man who had sent the Raiders to our farm was buying these men off and threatening to do bodily harm to the others. We found they had controlled this marker for some time. He would just now putting pressure on us. We had no idea as why as yet. Our men and the Sheriff have been watching him, he always had a couple of bodyguards around him all the time. Chuck Chum and I decided we would have to do something drastic. Chum and I were always looking for an improvement in our rifles and firearms. We came across an air rifle that would shoot with very little noise and was very accurate. The stock was used as the air chamber. It would reload and shoot numerous times with out pumping up the chamber. Chuck chum and I were amazed at this rifle. I told Chuck and chum this man is doing his best to do us in, he has sent assassins more than once and will try again. I told Chuck and chum I would change into city close to hide my identity and would find his routine and would ambush him with this rifle. I felt it was self-defense he was trying his best to do us in. This was to be Just between us. Told Jan mom and Sue and Bess I had needed to go to the city to attend some of my personal finances. Jan knew something was up, she knew all my finances had been in order when last in the city. Ended up having to tell her about what we had planned. She wasn't very happy about it, her comment was be dang careful. Had Jan help me with different clothes so no one would recognize me in the city. Was going to take a small carriage but change my mind. We have to park it somewhere would be too obvious. Would use one of our horses and would change often. the ride into the city was uneventful. Chuck told me where to go and stable my horse. They would not know me especially with my change of clothes. Did a lot of walking and observing. Had not found a good place to get to him as yet. He always seemed to be with some of his cronies. One afternoon seen him take a carriage and head out, walk very fast not running to see if I could find where he was heading. It looked as though he was heading out of the city I was disgusted with myself for not having a horse close by but felt there would be another time. Headed back to my lodgings upset with my poor planning. Had my evening meal at a restaurant, Chuck said he would meet me there. He would have any details I would need to know halfway through my meal Chuck walked in and came over and sat down. Well bird you can go back to the farm it's all taken care of. My quarry had left in his carriage to meet some woman out of town. Apparently something spooked his horse and it was a disaster for him the horse going full tilt where the wheels hit a stone and broke sending the carriage cart wheelling throwing him out. He didn't recover from the tumble, the horse also had to be put down. What a relief this was for me, told Chuck farm here I come. Chuck said he was going to look at buying out his estate and then reselling it, He would talk it over with mom Sue and Jan Chum and myself. He figured this would be a good way to control someone from trying to gouge us again. We could keep enough control so such moves would not be against us again. When I got back to the farm Jan pulled me into the bedroom to get all the information. She didn't know what had actually happened, relating what happen could see the relief in her eyes and posture. She then said how glad she was I didn't have to shoot. Of course she asked if I had anything to do with the wheel breaking on the carriage, laughing told her had seen the carriage when he left in it. I also told her was glad I didn't have to shoot the son of a gun. Less than a month later Chuck said he had made a deal with the estate. They had made a ridiculous price Chuck made a counteroffer that to him was also ridiculous. He said he then just turned and walked out. He never made it to where his horse was stable. When someone came running after him with please come back. They came back with a counter offer. Chuck being upset got up telling them his offer stood. They could find someone else to buy it out. They then had a confab and came back saying they would take his offer. Chuck had made up his mind to stick with his offer. They just wanted to get out the hassle of running the business. Chuck knew a few good men he could trust to run this business. He also told them they would be buying into the business and would share the profits. How lucky was our family Chum and I were to have Chuck with a his city know how. Chum and I would have just given up the deal. Back at the farm the babies were creeping all over wouldn't be long they would be walking. Guy Chuck chum and I were enjoying the babies. The two were inseparable they always wanted be together. When picking one up and sitting on your lap the other was there wanting to get up to. Then the tussle would start just a good natured tussle they were never mean to each other. Would always find them after their scampering around would be nestled together. The talk of a war hadn't affected us that much. Our farm and village was off the beaten path so to speak, we had not been involved that much. We were warned we might be raided at any time, fortunately we never were. Shared a lot of our news in the city, some of the village boys and Chuck was the one that had kept track of things. Chuck and mom back from the trip to the city had a surprise for Chum and myself. They had three Henry rifles. We were amazed at the work of this lever action rifle. Had tried out right away the cartridges were also well-made we found occasionally they would misfire and by turning the cartridge a quarter turn it would fire then. Found to be quite accurate also we made up carrying cases for our horses. We already had them made but we had to make adjustments to fit the new rifle. Couldn't help think of my Indian brothers how much easier it would make their hunting. Chuck told me they were very expensive most could not afford them. Our trading post had been doing well with the trade goods. The pelts were well received the city. The Buffalo hides were being overloaded, the prices of them had fallen way off. Sent word to the trading post to not take in any more Buffalo hides from any white man. Just the Indians. Chum was sorry hadn't come on our expedition out West he had made a few comments of how sorry he was he had not went with us. I told him I was going to make a trip again even if I went along his next comment was you won't be alone. Just couldn't get the rifles off my mind find. Finally asked Chuck could he get six more than. He smiled said thinking of your Indians brothers. He wasn't sure but thought he may be able get more with plenty of ammo for them. I never thought of the cost. Chum said Bird, Chuck took the money out of his account. When I approached Chuck he laughed and said he came out of our general fund of our joint account. As a couple of weeks or so before Chuck came back from the city with our rifles and wooden boxes to protect them. Jan knew I was planning take the rifles out to my Indian family. She wasn't too happy about it, she felt it was too dangerous we had been hearing strange stories about problem with the Indians. I felt it was problem with our people moving in on them. Treaties had been made and I thought that would settle things down. I then told Jan I would deliver the rifles and then not stay. This would most likely be my a last excursion West. Our man that was taking care of our trading post were doing quite well for us we had agreed for them to take a share in the profits which we kept for them he had married an Indian girl and was quite happy. It was late spring Chum and I had gotten ever thing ready for our excursion West. Jan and Sue weren't very happy about our going, both knew we had made up our minds to go and had they insisted we would not go but we wouldn't be very happy either. We told them we'd be back before summer's end. Chum was really excited about going, he had told me numerous times how we should have gone with us. He said it would have been a second honeymoon for him and Sue. We took six horses two pack horses and each a spare for riding. The trail was now well-established, the route have been change occasionally to make going a lot easier. We said our goodbyes with a lot of hugs Jan and Sue stated to be real careful. Then saying to me don't take any unnecessary chances. I promise I wouldn't then we were off we took our time enjoying the scenery and our companionship we hadn't done this type of togetherness for some time. We were always very close, was a great feeling for both of us. As we approached our trading post could see smoke. Told Chum something isn't right. Let's hobble the horses away from the trail and then go investigate. We took our time keeping a close watch for anything out of the ordinary. About a half-mile from the trading post someone called our names from the woods. Judd and his Indian bride came out of the woods to greet us. We found the post have been raided the two men that were there had been killed and a post burned after being ransacked.

43

Judd said he and his woman were out looking for tubers and things to eat when they heard the shooting. They were very cautious on going back. He observed six men, two maybe three were Indians the others were white man. They didn't get all the horses some had broken out of the corral and were around somewhere. Judd said he was looking for them when we came into view. We then went back to our horses and gear told Judd and his woman to wait we would go and investigate make sure it was safe to go back. Both chum and I rode for a ways and dismounted to go through the woods. Keeping to cover we made a circle around the post and found no one there. They had left taking whatever they could carry. The post was destroyed. Two men they had killed were mutilated. We would take time to give them a decent burial after finding the other horses and letting Judd and his bride know it was safe. We went looking for the other horses and were able to corral three. Then headed back to our gear and Judd and his woman. Judd still had his rifle, he said he always took it with him at any time he left the post. He was going to shoot one of the men but his woman stopped him. She knew they wouldn't survive if he had, I and Chum agreed. We made camp where we were next we had to decide what to do next. We determined that Judd and his woman will go back to the farm. They could tell Chuck and all what had happened. Judd wanted to go with us his woman and said okay but Chum and I insisted they both come back to the farm. Reluctantly they had agreed. Next day got the horses for Judd and his woman and sent them on their way. Chum and I went back to the post. We had already made a circle and found the trail which was well traveled. Following on foot we found they had split up, three had gone in a different direction the others were on the trail we would be using. Went back for our gear and horses, started up the trail keep them a sharp lookout. Also keeping track when they would with the three would camp or leave the trail. We found where they had camped, their sign was fresh. They all of a sudden left the trail. Must have heard us behind them. Told Chum we would walk beside her horses not giving them a good target. Told Chum I was getting a little careless. Started looking for a good place to stop. We needed cover of some kind I knew they would try to ambush us if we stayed on the trail. We came to ravine this is a good spot for us to stop. Told chum to get up on the next ridge I would get up on the other. I knew they would try to get above us they didn't know we had Henry rifles. When we separated I told Chum if he spotted them to shoot even if he didn't have a good shot they would expect only one shot. When they showed themselves your next shot would do the man in , don't hesitate. I had tied a couple of pots on our one of our pack horse to make them noise if we were getting ready for our meal heard a shot from chum side then another quiet then another and then another again. Had been watching another approaching from my side, he had his rifle up and ready, my one shot dropped him. Just in case my shot wasn't true went from tree to tree didn't need to but best to make sure. Left him and went to check on Chum. He was fine he had to shoot 3×1st shot had done one in. He had moved for the puff of smoke gave his place away the other man had shot at where he thought Chum was. Chum's next shot downed him. He was still moving Chum gave him another shot. When I went back to check on Chum he was watching for me. He had heard my shot and was sure it was from the new rifles we were using. He was sure was me that shot. Chum hollered okay over here, I then hollered back to let him know I was okay. Chum then asked me if we were going to bury them. I smiled and answered out here I'm an Indian. We will strip them and leave them face down. We then went and settled our mounts and pack horses. Went back to find their horses. Found they also had two pack horses from the raid on our post. This left us with five more horses chum suggested we just take everything with us and give or trade with the Indians. Just couldn't leave the goods and horses. Next morning we were on our way again occasionally could see were some digging was being done. We finally came across a couple of men, they told us they were prospector. I told them they were in Indian land wouldn't be very happy to find them their. They just laughed and said they could take care of themselves. I knew they were in danger of losing their lives. Still he just shrugged and grinned.

Another day went by we were getting ready to pack up when we heard horses coming. Was glad to see Indians that I knew and knew me. We had a good rapport they were heading for our post to trader hide. I told them that the post was raided and burnt. Also we had killed three of the men who were in on the raid and had what they had taken from us. One of the Indians next, not good to go against Brave Hawk.

We made our trade with them. We decided to stash the hides as best we could. Hung them in Buffalo hides up as high as we could would pick them up on our way back. My Indian friends were sure who the others were and they were Indians from another tribe. They decided to travel back to the encampment, they had been trapping for some time and would be glad to have us travel with them. Another few days or so and we would be out on the plains. We were just packing up for the day when 6 Sioux Warriors rode into our camp. Seeing us white men they weren't very cordial. Our Indians told them why was in that my trading trading post had been burnt out. They calm down when they told them I was there brother. We were looking for White Cloud and Gonacheaw and little arrow. They had stopped at the camp it was less then a day's ride. This was good news for Chum and me. This Sioux told us that men were coming into their sacred grounds and they were in the process of hunting them out. They had already eaten so didn't partake in our meal. I told them in their language Chum and I would be going back east before too long. We were here to tell the Chief that the trading post was no more. I had gifts for them also. We had rifles hidden I wasn't sure but was going to take any chances. Not knowing these 'Sioux. They left then we were on our way again. Before the day was done we had rolled into the encampment. Chief and my brothers were also there. They had been discussing the hunt they said they were having a hard time finding Buffalo. The white men were killing and just taking the hides. They welcome Chum like a brother I had to interpret for him. Next morning got the rifles out and showed them to the chief and the rest, then showed how they work. I said this will make your hunting a lot easier. The Chief said we haven't anything to trade and would not have enough items.. I said you gave me a tomahawk that save my life many moons ago. This is a very small exchange for that. He smiled. Little arrow also said he didn't have anything, I laughed and told him years ago you also gave me my life. You warn me when the Indians was going to shoot me. He then said you knocked arrows out of the air. My answer was the warning you gave me was what saved my life. He then smiled and nodded. Now Gonacheaw was grinning he knew I would come up with something so he wouldn't have to trade. I told him he taught me how to track and also not to get caught in an ambush plus willing to save me at the lake. Shook his head and hand me this very fancy tomahawk. I was shocked knew how much he liked this weapon. He could see the shock on my face, grinning said we now trade. He then grabbed my shoulder and gave me a shake. Chum didn't know what was happening, had to explain what was going on. We sat and had a good meal that the woman had prepared. Then little arrow said he had seen fresh buffalo sign or herd of of just so many just losing his hands to show how many. Plan the hunt for the next day. I then asked about my Indian mother. They told me she left the world sometime before. All the older woman I had known had left the world. One of the older woman from one of the close tribes came to me and told me her Shaman said I had much magic and no one would kill me. She then said I see it is true. We all were getting older the chief had white in his hair now. This also was a shock to me. The next day Chum and I relaxed and enjoyed a day of leisure. Little arrow said that he and Gonacheaw were planning a hunt. Chum had never been on a hunt before, he was looking forward to going. Some of the other Braves were not back from their hunt for Buffalo. Little arrow and Gonacheaw wanted to try out the new rifles. The chief was going to wait for the rest of the Braves come back, if they had luck they would pack up and go to harvest the buffalo. Just the four of us headed out to locate the buffalo little arrow had located. We found them late morning, it was a real large heard they weren't moving very fast. Little Arrow and I Went to One Side Gonacheaw and Chum on the other. The minute we showed ourselves they started to run. Little arrow rode in and caught up and fired downing one, then road a little further and downed another.

I didn't plan on shooting so just rolled up to where little arrow was. He turned to go to the last buffalo he had shot as I rode up a shot rang out and little arrow fell off his horse. I went to turn when the second shot hit me in the leg and went threw into my horse. My horse went down, was able to scramble out from under. Could see no movement from little arrow. Knew I had to move to cover, little arrows horse was still standing. My right leg was paralyzed, worked myself over to little arrows horse, then stood on my good leg grabbed the horses main and vaulted on with my rifle still in my hand. Whacked the horse in the rear with my rifle and he took off at a gallop. Another shot rang out but missed. Road into a shallow Gully then stopped. I knew Gonacheaw would know that something wasn't right. Chum and Gonacheaw stopped and headed for cover also. Wasn't long before Gonacheaw and Chum showed up. I was bleeding from the leg, my trousers were saturated. When Gonacheaw saw this he immediately had me take off my pants. He knew to wrap it to stop the bleeding, he then had me stand on it to make sure the bullet had not broken the bone. The feeling was coming back and the bone was not broken. Gonacheaw knew without asking that little arrow was dead. Gonacheaw said we should have scouted the whole area. We now knew there were buffalo hunters waiting for the herd to come into their range. We spoiled their hunt and they took out their anger by shooting us. We knew better than to go where little arrow was down. Could tell Gonacheaw was already planning, I was now able to walk the feeling was almost all back. Gonacheaw said for us to wait here with the horses he was going on foot to see where they these men were. Less than an hour or so he was back. They had a wagon and had packed up and were in the process of leaving. Gonacheaw went on foot to intercept them, we were to follow behind to keep their attention. This took part of the afternoon. I kept getting off my horse to keep my leg from setting up. Chum just shook his head wondering how I was able to do it. Finally seen one man drop off the wagon with his rifle. He was planning on ambushing us, told Chum to take the horses and head into the gully. Would wait for him on foot. We next heard a shot out front, knew this was Gonacheaw. The one shot was all we needed to know one man was down. The man who had planned on ambushing us hollered for the wagon to stop he ran to it and climbed on. Then the driver beat the horses into a run, another shot and the wagon went tumbling sideways and rolled over and over. Chum and I went back and then got our horses. Two more shots and another. This Chum and I knew was from our new rifles. Gonacheaw was waiting for us, all four men were dead. Gonacheaw had shot one horse and when it fell causing the wagon to roll and tumble. Before we got there, there was another shot. The other horse was also badly hurt so Gonacheaw put it down also. We gathered up everything and started all their equipment on fire. The men were stripped and left face down. We then went back to get Little Arrow. I had a hard time looking at him. This in my younger brother he had always looked up to me. A better friend or brother couldn't ask for. Chum and I felt the same about each other. Had to shoot my horse he could not get up the bullet had broken his back what a horrible day. I was going to walk along with Gonacheaw, we just had the three horses. Little Arrow was on Gonacheaw 's horse. Gonacheaw insisted I ride, then walk a little but not to start the bleeding again. I took his advice. When we got back to the village Little Arrows woman couldn't believe he had been killed. The other hunters were back without any luck, we had four Buffalo down. The camp was moved to where the buffalo were. I then realize how low they were on food. The Chief said many white men killed just for the hide. The grieving started after the camp was set up again. A week went by very slowly. Chum and I and the whole tribe were very down. I knew we would be leaving to go back in a short while. We talk with the Chief and Gonacheaw about our post being burned down. We were the only ones that didn't have firewater for trade. Also they knew they would not be cheated. There shaman who is now a younger man looked at my leg and gave me some herbs to put on the wound. The bullet had went through my leg and into my horses breaking his back. Still had my other pony my filly's second colt, it was hard to lose a brother and one of my favorite ponies at the same time. Gonacheaw told us that this new rifle had let him take care of these men. With out the rifle he would've had a lot harder time and would have taken a lot more time. We weren't only a few days ride from the Black Hills. Told the chief would try to set up another post. His comment was we need the post it was always fair. Your men never took advantage of would not trade firewater. Gonacheaw also commented the buffalo were getting harder to find because of the white men. Heading back was much easier, we didn't have any goods to worry about. Gonacheaw came with us he wanted to leave some of the little arrows things at our first village. He said this was some of the happy times, he also stated he still had never figured out how he was never able to track me down. I was the only one that he was never able to track. I told him it was meant to be it was our spirits. He also acknowledge this. The only shaman had decided to go also. He caught up with us after the first day. He told us that he would have a ceremony over Little Arrows things. We were into the Black Hills and getting close to our first village. We met up with six Sioux Indians, they weren't happy to see two white men in our group.

When I started talking in an Arapaho and also in their language their attitude change. One said I know you Brave Hawk, see you when you kill the one who challenged you many moons ago. Was one of the Braves with big Tomahawk and he didn't die well. Gonacheaw just grinned and acknowledged him. We then told them what had happened to my brother little arrow I also said that Gonacheaw done all four in, they were glad to hear this. They were here to drive out some white men who weren't supposed to be on their land. Two of the Sioux Indians we met wanted to see the scars from my fight. Gonacheaw made me know to do this. The scars from my bear encounter were still quite prominent also the scar my ribs from the fight with the Pawnee. They nodded and told me, you have a powerful spirit. The stories also seem to get embellished. The actual fight lasted about a minute after big Tomahawk stepped into the circle. The story was it now lasted half a day. Was hard for me to believe that they had heard about this encounter also about how I escaped. This is why they said I had a powerful spirit. On parting they said tell anyone you see to leave our land. Will kill them if they stay I Then Told Them Chum and I Had told two men they had best leave or suffer the wrath of the Indians. I knew they didn't pay any mind to us. My leg was doing real well had scabbed over and wasn't near as painful. Another half day and Gonacheaw and I found the remnants of our original village. He said to me very happy here. I felt the front of emotions with my memories and had to turn away, he just nodded. I knew it was one of the happiest times for me. Was now very happy with my life with Jan and the new daughter. The shaman held his ceremony and we did some dancing to his chanting after the ceremony that lasted into the night, we all slept well. Chum had even got up and danced with us. Gonacheaw and I were pleased he did. Gonacheaw then told me he would make a good Indian. Chum's chin dropped he didn't expect such a compliment. I just grinned and said he was always an Indian just like I was. Chum then just laughed and gave me a pat on the back next morning we said our goodbyes. The shaman said we will meet again in the spirit world, Gonacheaw just smiled. Gonacheaw also said keep your rifles hid many will kill for them. We had kept our rifles in their leather scabbards when we had met the six Sioux Indians, was glad we did. They would have wanted to trade for them and we would have had to refuse. This wouldn't have gone over very well. Knowing this Sioux they would more than likely have set an ambush up somewhere in order get them. As we passed through the rest of the Black Hills ran into quite a few men all were prospectors. The word had gotten out some had found gold. I also warned them they were on Indian land. They want to know what we were doing in their land. I informed them I was Indian and they knew me quite well. Come to visit my brother and he was killed by buffalo hunters. Also told him the four of them were buzzard bait now. Let them know the Sioux were already in the area. This didn't seem to bother him very much. Chum and I could see a lot of problems ahead. We found the hides we had hid earlier and packed them with us. We got back to where our trading post had been, the barn wasn't damage but would be a lot of work setting up again. Chum and I talked it over and decided not to bother we had enough going on at the farm in the sawmill. We were back at the farm a little ahead of schedule. Was great to see everyone Jan give me a huge hug, step back and said look like you and Chum at a hard time. I was going to disagree when Chum spoke up and told Jan and Sue my Indian brother had been killed in a buffalo hunt by buffalo hunters. He then also added Bird was also shot. I just commented our trip could have been better. The Indians are getting really upset about the men coming into the Black Hills their land. We asked if Judd his woman had got to the farm okay. Mom spoke up she said set them up in one of our small cabins. They were both now working on the farm. Chuck would be do back from the city anytime. The and help had two wagon loads of farm produce for the city. Mom said Chuck was also thinking of moving lumber to the city. Lumber was at a premium.

Chuck showed up just at suppertime, he was very glad to see us. He said he really needed our help a lot more than we realize. Now we could help take the load off of him. Running everything was a lot of work the last two months was busy getting produce to the city. We needed to check out the sawmill something didn't seem to be quite right. At Supper Chum and I Had to Relate Everything about Our Trip. Mom Jan Bess and Sue all piped up and said we hope this is your last trip to West. I agreed that things had change so much in just a short time. This time out found the buffalo was there main source of food. The buffalo hunters were just killing and just taken the hide. We had seen a whole herd slaughtered just rotting away. I could see a hard time for the Indians if this kept up. I tried to think of anything I could do to help stop the killing of the buffalo. Chuck and Chum said it was the times changing not much we could do. You could speak up for all the good it would do in the city they were too busy with their own agendas Chuck said he hadn't had time to check out on the sawmill, seem like they were having some trouble. Chum said bird and I will see what is going on and iron things out. The next day we went to see Judd in his woman, they were glad to see us. Judd then told us that a couple of men had gone up to the mill that he didn't like. He said he knew one of them from the trading post and he had a real mean streak. Told Chum that's all we need. When we left things were going real well. Bess's little boy Chad and my daughter Laura Lee were already starting to walk a lot of love and enjoyment with these two toddlers running around. When left to themselves it would always be found together. Told Jan once we found out what was going on at the mill would like to spend time at the lake. Bess asked if she could join us, both Jan and I agreed and told her she didn't have tor ask she was always welcome. Chum and I headed to the mill we decided to not just walk in but to observe from a distance see if we could find anything out of the place. First thing when found our foreman was nowhere to be seen. This is very strange to us. Then a strange man we knew we hadn't hired seem to be acting like the foreman. We went back to the farm to check to see if Chuck had hired different help. Mom said no definitely not also the lumber proceeds were not coming in. We headed back up and walked into the mill. We accosted these two men asking the others where our foreman was. No one answered us, we then could tell these two men had taken over the mill. Next one of the men said were running the mill now. I just said okay and motioned Chum we would leave, we backed out of the mill. Went to our horses and left, didn't go far, just far enough to get out of sight. We also had observed two or three other strangers, our original help seem scared by these men. Chum told me he would go back with his rifle on the ready. I was to go to the side and cover him. Chum walked in and accosted the one that had claimed to be running the mill. He told him and he was to leave. The man turned and swung back with a pistol in his hand. Chum was ready and shot as he ducked to evade the pistol. The other man I was holding at gunpoint. He now looks scared his attitude had change in a hurry. The other strangers just stood with their eyes wide. I then asked where our foreman was and are other help. The two men that were still on our payroll then spoke up telling us these men said they were hired to take over the mill. The foreman had resisted and they had not seen him since the other men had taken over the mill. The other men said they had been hired by the man that we had just killed and didn't know about what was going on. The other man when asked just shrugged his shoulders. Pulled my knife and had it as throat still no answer. I had the two of our original man start the saw. Chum knew what was planned. He wrapped the guy aside the head we tied his hands and feet to the carriage. Started him into the blade with his feet toward the blade. He could see the look in our eyes we meant to slice him ass first threw the saw. He then began to talk almost crying. They had taken our foreman out and had beaten him. He was gone the next morning another one of the men was giving him a hard time and we just killed him. Most of our original help had been driven off. The men they had hired decided to leave, we scared the hell out of them. This accomplice had helped with the beating and murder of one of our help. I was going to take them out and just shoot him. Chum said, Chuck is Sheriff let him handle this part. We asked our original help if they knew where the others were. One answered the foreman was staying with his family in the village and recovering from the beating. We would see if we could locate the rest of our help and will go and check on our foreman. Had them shut things down until we were organized again. We would haul this man down and keep him for trial and the village. We then untied the other man's feet, he said you would have run me threw that saw. My answer was you know damn well I would have. I put a rope around his neck and headed for the farm. His hands are still tied. We put him in the Barn had Judd keep an eye on him I told Judd if he gives you a hard time just shoot the so-and-so. After we left he told Judd he knew he would be hung but it was a lot better than being sawed into in that saw blade. Next we went to look up our foreman. He was recovering and was fortunate to survive. Broken arm in two places plus being beaten unconscious. He knew we had to get away so he had made it to the village. He was very confused and was just getting back his memory. He was afraid they would kill all of his family. When he heard that one was dead and the other was captured could see the relief in his face. Our foreman and other workers thought we had sold the mill to them. Our foreman said he knew where the other men were and he would round them up to go back to work. We had lost business because these men demanded payment before the work was being done. There wasn't any sawmill like ours within miles. When the customers found out what had happened they were back in droves. We had always been fair in our pricing. Sometimes you would take a pig , chickens or a cow in trade, then off to the city to sell them. Most well to do didn't grow or raise any of their own produce. Chuck said he knew something was wrong but had so many other things going he hadn't had time to check it out. Mom and Sue hadn't said anything because Chuck has so many other things going. He was glad we were back from our trip to help run things again. The farm was also doing real well. This and other holdings in the city kept Chuck busy. He now could relax and he and mom are going to the city to enjoy and relax for a couple of weeks. A lot of friends and partying was a welcome change every so often. Chum and I spent quite a lot of time getting the mill back to the good running order. Then we started on the farm, we were fortunate to have good help. They lived on the farm in cottages we had built for them. Getting to look like a small village. At harvest time we would hire boys or girls from the village if any were available. Most were quite young, the older boys went to the city to seek their fortune. Chum and I hadn't had time to talk about our time with the Indians. So we related all that had happened. Chum telling about Little arrow being shot, also said Bird was fortunate he was just wounded but his pony was killed with the same shot. He and Gonacheaw are on the other side of the buffalo herd. They all looked at me and wanted to know what had happened. Told him it all happened quite fast. One shot had gotten Little Arrow the second hit me and my pony. Little arrows pony had just stood there. I rolled holding onto my rifle and found one leg had no feeling. Got close to little arrows pony and managed to get on his back and then started him on the run. Another shot was fired but had missed me. Chum and Gonacheaw had swung back but stayed below the rise the, this is where I'd met them when I got off the little arrows pony, my leg was still numb and I almost fell. Lowered my pants to see how bad the wound was, I knew Gonacheaw was upset even though he didn't show this. We figure was buffalo hunters and we had spoiled their hunt. Gonacheaw checked my leg no broken bones the bullet went cleaned through and into my pony. Was now getting the feeling back. Wrap some of my linen underwear to stop the bleeding. Gonacheaw told us he would go on foot to head them off. I said we would follow on our ponies when Chum and

I had got near they had stopped their wagon, Chum and I just rode into a gully. They had long range rifles. We then heard a shot we know this was Gonacheaw with the new rifle. We then observe the other man run for the wagon. Gonacheaw had shot one man off his horse. When the other clambered into the wagon they had beat the horse into a gallop the next shot and the wagon went tumbling one horse was shot and caused the wagon to tumble. A few more shots and we knew none survived. When chum and I got to the wagon had to shoot the other horse also. All four men were dead we stripped the men and piled everything into the wagon burning it leaving all men face down. Headed back for Little Arrow, my pony was still alive and had to shoot him. his back had been broken by the shot. Chum knew how I felt about this pony and he offered to shoot him for me. He was just nickering, I went over and gave him a hug before I could put him down. The tribe was devastated by Little Arrows death. Move the village to where the buffalo were then the grieving began. This seem to take a toll on the whole tribe including myself. I couldn't believe that he had saved me and I wasn't able to do the same for him. I couldn't ask for any better brother. Chum fit in the same mold for me. We left the Indians and were anxious to get back to the farm. Jan and Bess both made the comment, they had noticed I was walking different. They just knew but couldn't figure out what it was. Mom then commented Bird how you have survive will never know. This got a chuckle at everyone. Everything was running smoothly again. Jan and Bess were planning our time at our lake. Bess said guy hadn't taken any time off from his work, she said he was waiting until we got back from the West. I talked Chum and Sue into also coming to Lake for a vacation. The cabin had been expanded to accommodate all of us. Chum had one of the men from the sawmill keep track of the place. He had no problems, he and his wife had taking care that everything was dusted and made sure no animals had gotten in. This would be another honeymoon for all of us. The weather was great, we fished swam and evenings playing cards would sing some of the songs that were popular at the time. The bugs during the day weren't much of a bother. Evenings the mosquito were a nuisance. We used oakum around the doors and windows also would burn candles with some kind of mixture mom and Sue had made up. This kept the bugs and mosquitoes at bay. We visited back and forth and then went back and got the two kids. They enjoyed the lake and the splashing in the water. Jan and Bess were in agreement they needed another baby. My filly had had another colt this time it was a filly. She was getting on in age so didn't think she would have another fold. This is when I missed my dog. We had got him back to the farm, he seemed to be recovering. Tried to follow me everywhere was having a hard time. I thought he was doing quite well for all his injuries from the fight. Short time later he came up missing, one of the farm help seen him head into the woods. Went looking for him took me a couple of days to find him. He had died and was just curled up in a ball. I buried him where he laid. Others had dogs on the farm but we never acquired another one. Maybe later if we ever found the right one. I knew would never be another like him. We all enjoyed our stay at the lake, we had not been that relaxed in a long time. Seemed good to have everything running smooth again. Chuck Chum and I had decided not to reopen the trading post again. Was getting to be too much of a hassle, a lot of the Indians wanted whiskey. This we would not do. We would have to move further west to establish a new post because the Indians had moved further west. We had enough going without that much of a hassle. The Army was also setting up outpost to protect the whites that were moving west. Could see a lot of conflict coming. A lot of whites were moving into the Black Hills, this was sacred land for the Indians. I understood there was a treaty of some sort. They army was supposed to keep the whites out, I just couldn't see this happening. Especially now let some of the stories of the gold being found. Gold craze set in. When things were quiet Jan asked me casually in my travels with the Indians was I ever tempted sleep with any of the Indian maids. I laughed and told her my first wife and Indian maid had died at childbirth. This I took very hard and planed on drowning myself in the lake we shared many a time. The old Shaman knew I was coming with my two Indian brothers following. He had somehow called me out of the lake and use some kind of smoke and Chanting to take the pain away. I didn't think I would ever marry again till meeting you. I had one maid approach me just stared at her she backed off in a hurry, as she looked back was still looking at her she just took off on the run. Two young Braves had seen this and commented I had a very powerful spirit. Another time when going to my sleeping place there was a maid wrapped up in my blankets I just flipped her out and went to another tepee with little arrow and his family. The woman got the message that I wasn't bothered again. Then I said if you were to leave me I wouldn't be here very long. You're more than enough for me. Jan's next words were let's go make a baby we both laughed and proceeded to do just that. Mom and Chuck and Sue Jan and Bess were talking about having Jan's father and also Bess's mom and dad come to the farm for a visit. We actually needed more room for extra people to be able to stay comfortably. We had been thinking about expanding but plans had not been made up as yet. Chum and I had been busy at the sawmill and other prospects on the farm, seems like always something to iron out. We both enjoyed our work a challenge was always looked at as a learning experience. Mom and Chuck were planning the party for Jan's father Bess's father and mother also Guys mom and dad. Mom insisted Lora lee sleep in her and Chuck's room. Chuck was back from the city everything was going real well our goods were well received. At times he said he could have double the prices, he knew none of us would have wanted that. His next suggestion was why don't Chum and you plan on another addition for our guest. So the planning began with all making suggestions. We finally settle on a set of plans including an outhouse not too far away. A second outhouse would be so no one would have to wait. We had our bathing room in the main house, would plan on another in the guest addition. With help from the farm and sawmill, wasn't long before the foundation was down in the building started. We decided also to make a walkway to the new outhouse. This would accommodate the whole house rather than just the guest rooms. In inclement weather much more comfortable to be able to walk without getting rained on or getting rain gear on to make a deposit. we ran out of nails we were using for our boarding. Set one of our men to the city to get more we ordered a full keg of nails very expensive but much easier to build with. We had made a lot of our own but very time-consuming. The city blacksmith shop for using balls after finding the right metal mixture that wasn't brittle as cast-iron. We were still drilling and pegging our main beams. Chum and I devised a power drill at the mill to drill the beams. This made things go much faster, they were all drilled with a jig that guided each hole so all were consistent. Made a big difference in the speed of our construction with double boarding on the outside and single on the inside. This made for a lot warmer in the winter and with the cellar cooler in the summer. The party was happening before we had all the construction finished. Everyone invited knew we were in the process of expanding our home and they said they didn't mind a little inconvenience. Mom Sue Jan and Bess were excited about having our friends coming for stay. Chum Sue Jan Bess and I were making sleeping places in one of the barns we used for storing grain hay etc. the smell was quite pleasant. We didn't mind the smell of the horse barns either. Just easier to set up temporary places to sleep. Chad and Laura Lee enjoyed the grain in the hay barn also. They could play without getting into too much trouble. Mom was like an old mother hen keep an eye on them most of the time. They always managed to escape her attention. They just wanted to explore everything getting into mischief every so often. Jan Bess and I always took them on horseback, both kids really looked forward to our rides. We took them up to our lake quite often. This had become one of our favorite spots to get away from the turmoil of the farm and sawmill. We now had a couple of rowboats and a canoe. The fishing was still excellent. By keeping out the people who were using net's and other means to catch large quantities of fish stopping this kept the fishing great. Both Laura Lee and Chad enjoyed the fishing they also loved playing in the water. Wouldn't be long before they would be swimming, they were both now talking. I still daydreamed occasionally about my time with the Indians and disliked the way they were now being treated. The newspapers are always telling about horrible things they were doing. Nothing about the terrible things were doing to them. The Black Hills was one of their sacred places. Heard that the treaty was now being ignored. The land was supposed to be theirs. The word was gold had been found, I knew that greed would take over. I would try to let everyone know about the things were going to the Indians. Most of the time would get very negative reactions. Any news was about how terrible the Indians were. Had to refrain from this as would have had many fights and a lot of hard feelings. Even some of our friends were convinced of the word that was being passed around as news. I would mention we were invading their land, what would we do if they were invading our land. This had no effect on anyone I had talked to even though they had brought up the subject. The buffalo were being slaughtered just for their hides the carcass were just left there to rot. Would mention if our food sources being destroyed wouldn't we fight like hell to stop the destruction. Most would ignore me from then on, just didn't want to hear this.

We had everything just about ready for visiting friends, this included the bankers and their wives. Chuck told chum and me we should go to the city to see the bankers. They wanted us to check out our private accounts to our satisfaction also theirs. Chuck knew I wasn't overly anxious about what was what was going on. He came and asked me if I would please go, I had to agree. He had done so much for us just couldn't refuse them. Chuck said he had some accounts he had to take care of, we would make the rounds together. We knew we would be invited to different places for dinners. Chuck asked me not to get into any discussion about the Indians, this would just cause a lot of problems for us. I made the promise would not bring any of my feelings up about how the Indians were being treated. Jan said Bird we know the truth because of your knowledge but others will not see it our way, so don't even bring up the subject. If they do please ignore it please. I will was my promise we all rode our horses. We used one large wheeled wagon just to carry our tent and cooking supplies. This made for a pleasurable trip. One of our young men working on the farm volunteered to drive our two wheeled cart. On our way we had caught up to two large wagons. When we passed realized they were loaded with just buffalo hide. This left me with a very down and disgusted feeling, I knew I couldn't do much about it. Jan noticed my different demeanor and asked what was wrong. Told her that the large wagons were loaded with just buffalo hides. I knew the carcasses were left to rot, this was the Indians food source. They didn't waste anything all was used. Jan said Bird you have to let it go. You're just one person against many who are convinced Indians are horrible people. We know better but just bringing it up cause us a lot of trouble and hard feelings. I know was my answer also wish I could do something for them. Wasn't long after quite a few days on the trail we were in the city. We went to the inn we always stayed at. We're always treated very well, we had stayed there for quite a few years. Word got out we were in the city and the dinner invites came in. We let Sue Jan and Bess do all the answering to the invites. Mom had insisted she was going to stay home and watch our two rascals. We had planned on bringing them with us, but mom put her foot down and that was the way it was going to be. Chuck was a little disappointed mom was staying behind. Jan Bess and I knew the girls and women on the farm would have been happy to take care of the two kids. Our first evening we just had a leisurely meal at the end. A lot of friends were there also, some ate there regularly. Others heard we were there and came just to be in on the conversation that was going on. A few tried to get me to talk about what was happening out West. My comment was I just didn't really know. This satisfied most. Made up mind not to be led into any discussions on the subject. Knew I would get carried away and just hard feelings would ensue. There was no way of changing any minds about how we were the ones that were treating the Indians badly. Next day we rode our horses out to Guys father's place on the lake was quite pleasurable, the caretakers were doing a very good job. One of their sons was also there. He did a lot of the repairs and upkeep, he also acted as a good guard. When Guys dad found out he insisted on paying him. His comment he was just happy to have a place to stay. I told Jan want to go and see my blacksmith friends, had been quite a while. Jan came with me. On the way we passed a large warehouse, I spotted the two wagons that that have been caring the buffalo hides. Jan and I were curious to see what else was in the warehouse. We stopped and it was hard to believe it was filled with nothing but buffalo hides. The men told us they would be shipped east and sent to England. I made the comment that there would have been enough meat to feed the city for a year, shook my head and commented that meat was just left to rot. The man just shrugged his shoulders. We then headed for the blacksmith shop. We found a lot of improvements, the men that I knew now just supervise the shop. They were now living quite well from their profits. They also payed their men quite well. Found they were also experimenting with ways of making different metals and had some good results. They were making a lot of nails, had a constant call for them. They had made split mold and poured into these with good results. Headed back to the end and got ready for for dinner outing. Jan Bess Guy Chum Sue and I spent the afternoon at a theater that had a comedy skit going. We met a lot of acquaintances that were glad to see us. Some were invited to the dinner that we were also invited to. Everyone enjoyed the comedy we headed back to the inn and relaxed before getting ready for dinner invite. Jan and I had planned on walking, our plans were changed when a carriage arrived to take us to our destination. I of course went in my buckskin clothes. Chum said I know bird you will never wear any of the dress closes even mom would like to see you in. Jan just chuckled, her, comment was I wouldn't even recognize my own husband. We all got a big laugh out of that. We arrived at our destination were escorted into the main dining hall. This was early evening a group of musicians had been hired. Bess and Guy were already there, the dancing began with one of the musician directing. Jan was a very good dancer and Sue insisted that I learn. We had practice at the farm quite often, after the evening meals. Chuck chum and Sue joined the and they were all very good dancers. Didn't take me only a short time to be doing real well. I felt bad mom was not with us to enjoy the festivities. There were drinks for both the ones that refrained from any alcohol beverages also plenty of other drinks without alcohol. Jan and I would only drink a glass of wine. Chum and Sue were also only wine consumers. We also never drank to excess. I had done this once when younger and made up my mind would never do it again. Very sick for the next day and more, the heck with that. Chum Sue Jan and I danced every dance. Some different men would approach Jan Bess and Sue and asked them to dance. Bess and Guy would exchange partners, but both being from the city knew who were gentlemen and ladies. Jan and Sue turned down all advances. Some and I would wander off to join the men, the girls would do the same could catch up on all the local gossip with the ladies Jan had one man insists she dance with him. She just stared him down, he finally left her alone. This get-together was put on by our banker friends and some of their friends. Jan's father and also Guys and Bess's mom and dad. Late evening the meal was served. Everything was excellently prepared and served. We had just finished our meal when to policeman showed up looking for me. Couldn't figure out what they wanted. Found out the warehouse we had stopped at was burning. Because Jan and I had stopped there earlier in the day, someone had said I had started the fire. Both the bankers then came to my rescue. They were very upset about the fire, that had contracted with someone to have the hides shipped east. Then also told the police I had an interest in the hides as well. I wasn't about to burn my own investment. Fortunately the fire had been put out before it got completely out of hand. We thought a lot of the hides might be ruined. Both of the bankers swore out arrest warrants for the contractor. He had been paid a portion of the fee to transport them East. The policeman said they would report back to their chief. Chuck hearing this went back with the police to straighten things out. He suspected the contractor thought I would be a good one to blame the fire on. He didn't realize I had an investment in the hides. One of the guards said he had seen me there. I was going to go back with Chuck. Chuck insisted I stay and enjoy the evening. He also said Bird you probably would cut the guards throat. The bankers let everyone know everything was settled and being taking care of. The evening went very well. Everyone wanted to know about the trip we had made out West to visit my Indian friends. I always call them my brothers. Jan was very good at narrating the happenings. She just had a wonderful way of telling a good story, she could embellish a little to really live in the story up. Especially about when I rescued her. Someone asked her if this really happened. She assured them it was probably a lot that was left out. How I had road into the group of men and hauled her onto my horse in one swoop. The group of men were struck dumb for a short time. The one I had run over wasn't getting up right away. These men were cutthroat, they would turn on anyone for a little profit. Jan also related how I had gone back and rounded up their horses so they would not be able to follow us. She's also said a lot of things had been left out. The girls and woman had asked if any of the men and harmed her. Her answer was I had rescued her before they had got to decide who was going to have her. The one that had grabbed her was stopping the rest of the men and was keeping her for himself. This is when I road into the group and ran over this guy with my pony and swinging her up onto my pony. She said she had wanted to go back with me. But Bird went on foot he was more Indian than I and could be very quiet. Also his dog was with him would give him warnings and also protection. The woman and girls were all looking at me with a very odd look. They told Jan your man just doesn't look that mean. Jan said he isn't only what he is crossed. I had to ask Jan and Bess what they had told the group woman and girls. Both just laughed and said the truth. I still didn't know what was going on, found both Bess and Jan to be good storytellers. Jan and Bess also told him what the Indians called me, Brave Hawk. They also wanted to know how I came about that name. They told them you would have to ask Bird. Next morning went with Chuck to the police station. We found out the guard that had accused me was the one who had set the fire. People that were living nearby had seen him pile kindling against the back wall and start the fire. He had not seen them and they were afraid the fire would also burn them out. They had rounded up others and had put the fire out before it got a real good start. A hard rain the day before had left much of the wood went so fire did a lot of smoldering but had done some damage most of the warehouse was saved. I was determined to find the help that put the fire out and pay them. The warehouse wasn't too far from the blacksmith shop, they already knew what had happened. The contractor had already fled town. They also knew who the guard was, he was still in the city. They told me he was the one I had met the day before at the warehouse. He was also stupid enough to try to use me as a culprit. He didn't realize I had an investment in the hides. When the police came looking for him he left in a hurry. I knew I could rely on the kids to help me locate him. Had befriended them quite a while back and had always gave them small sums for things I had asked them to do for me. They also had a good rapport with the men at the shop. I met them and asked if they knew where the guard was, they said no. But were sure they could locate him for me. I made up my mind he was not going to get away with accusing me then setting the fire himself. Wasn't just a couple of days when one of the boys was waiting outside the inn watching for me. He just waved and left. Jan asked me what was going on I tried to be evasive but she knew I was up to something. Had to tell her what was happening. She went with me to talk with the kids I had employed to find the guard. They also said he was with a bunch of men at a pub. he was buying two men drinks to keep an eye out for anyone that was asking about him. I couldn't get over how the kids had located him and also found out the other information. Jan said they know more of what's going on then police do. I said the police don't always treat them very good and they always clam up when asked about anything. When they like and trust you they will go out of their way for you. I then asked them to keep a lookout for him if he decides to change his whereabouts, they just nodded. I had Jan give them money and told the bigger boys to be honest and share. Jan asked if they were sharing with the two girls that were there. They just gave a shrug. Jan then went to the girls and gave them some coin, they were surprise. Jan found out the girls were the first to locate the guard then had told the boys. Now I had to plan on my next move. It definitely wasn't going to be in the daytime. Jan said she was not going to be left behind. Told Jan you know I can handle myself. Her answer was you could always use extra eyes and ears. I thought about calling it to a halt, Jan then said there just one guy and if we give the others coin they will also leave him. I would have to dress differently, my buckskin clothing would just give me away in a hurry. For the first time in a long while would dress in regular clothes for our escapade. We both would dress down to what the lower class wore. This way we wouldn't be noticeable. The kids we employed kept the watch and nothing had changed. They would leave the pub and separate at his dwelling. I told Jan have to catch him outside once in the place he's staying will make it too dangerous. He would know the lay out and we wouldn't. We decided to go out and act just like a couple out for a stroll. We had the kids helping us on the layout of the streets he and his friends took. It took us a couple of nights to lay out our plan. As we walk past the trio I would use a club to knock the guard down, then we would face off the other two toss them coin and hope they would accept and leave. Next night we set ourselves up for the confrontation, as we walk by was able lay a blow aside the guards head and he went down. This surprise the other two, they just stood dumbfounded. Jan told him we had coin for them to just leave. They both readily agreed. Two of the kids came with the rope we had given them. Tied the guard up and rolled him to the side of the road. I gave the boys my club, told him if he starts to roll give him a wrap and tell if he doesn't shut up he will be wrapped a lot harder. Jan and I went after our horses we had left at the stable not too far away. Now is the job of getting loaded on the back of my horse. He came around enough to ask what this was all about. He wasn't as heavy as I thought he was and had him laying across the back of our pony with not too much trouble. We then gave the kids that assisted us more coin. They said we had already paid them. We said this is for extra help you have given us also make sure you share and also with the girls. Jan will be upset if you don't. They agreed and left on the run, Jan I had to giggle at them. Was close to dawn when we arrived at the police station with our prize. The chief was surprised, he also said we need the two of you as our detectives. The guard was very subdued he said if you are employing people like this we will never get away with anything. The chief looked at us and just grinned. He knew word would get out and maybe some would think twice about pulling off such stunts. Jan and I headed back to the inn leaving our ponies at the stable the men there were surprised to see me dressed in clothes just like they wore. We were looking for a good breakfast and told them we would let them know what went on. When we got to the inn, they were also surprised to see me and Jan dressed in everyday workman's close. Jan's clothes were also in the work woman's. He thought we had gone to some kind of costume party. We sat down to breakfast and before we had our meal finish were being given some odd looks. Word had spread fast about us bringing the guard into the police. He was supposed to be a tough person. One of the maids said well he met more than his match this time. Chum and Sue wanted to know what the heck went on. Chum and Sue were upset with us for not informing them of what we had planned, Jan answered for us. She said if anything at all had gotten out of what we were planning the outcome could have been a lot different. Jan then said we just didn't think about telling anyone and were sorry we didn't say anything to you. Sue just grinned and said I knew Bird and Jan were up to something seem so secret I didn't want to interfere. We also found the bankers are a lot sharper than a contractor. The money set up to for him was on a small drive. He couldn't take only a small portion at a time and then only as he worked his way along the route he was supposed to take. So we only got away with a small amount. We found he had argued with one of the tellers to no avail. He was left with what little he was allowed to withdraw. The next thing Jan and I had to tell the bankers about our escapade and catching the guard who had set the fire. A planned another party but of just close friends at one of their homes. Jan and I had to go into hiding. We went to Jan's father place on the lake. Jan's dad had got together with the bankers and friends for another party. This time just close friends is hard to believe how fast news got out even the paper had a story about it. Not very accurate and very much embellished. Chum and Sue also came with Bess and Guy shortly. They said they were being pestered to know about what had happened. They said they didn't know either. Bess gave Jan a tongue lashing for not letting her know. They had never kept any secrets from one another. She just then laughed and gave Jan a big hug. Jan said everything happened so fast and with our planing we never thought about telling anyone. We are just thankful things went as well as we had planned even better. As to guard just left him without even any argument. The only secret we kept was how we had used the kids that I had made friends with two locate the guard. We knew that some of the people around them would not take what they did favorably. Jan and I talked it over and would tell everyone we had paid some contacts and we were on our word not to divulge them. Jan's father Henry talked Bess's mom and dad also Guys mom and dad and the two of our bankers and some of the other close friends to his home for the next dinner get together. Sue Chum Bess Jan and I were ready to head back to the farm. City life was okay but just not for us, this would be our last dinner before heading back to the farm. Everyone we knew would want to hear about our escapade. The evening went well the meal was again excellent. All were waiting for the meal to be over so our story would be told. Jan was a good storyteller she would only ask me to confirm or add to what she was telling. We agreed that everything went even better than what we had planned. They also wanted Jan Sue Bess to relate about our Western travel out West. They were never satisfied and wanted to hear about our travels out West. Jan Bess and Sue enjoyed talking about our Western escapade. Still others that hadn't been privy to the first telling of the guards capture wanted Jan and I to retell how we are able to capture the guard. Where we got our information from. Of course we would not divulge where it came from. Everyone was amazed at the things we did and accomplish. How we knew how to go about this they thought was them near impossible. The warehouse was not that badly damage. The bankers hired new help and supplies to repair the back wall. The hides were mostly smoked up with no fire damage. Having talked with a lot of the men about the news coming out to the West it was hard to believe some of the stories about how terrible the Indians were. I knew better and at times would interject how I felt. Relating they had a treaty and we were infringing and invading their territory. I always would say if they were infringing on our land we

70

would do the same if not worse. I found this was not well received by a good many of the men. Headed back to the farm, we were all anxious to be going home. The city was great for a short visit but a short visit was enough. Our friends and bankers had commented on how well they were received at our farm. They couldn't get over some of Chuck Chum and myself seeming inventions. Running water into the house, even our bathrooms had running water. Had to devise a system of get rid of the waste water also. We were quite comfortable some were wondering how they could get running water into their homes. Most had dug well so would be much more complicated than our system of Spring brook feeding our supply. Jan's father Henry was the only one who had a spring that was close to his home. Henry talked it over with us and we had agreed to help them with the project. He would hire help to do the digging and the set up at the spring. He wanted us just to supervise the endeavor. We told Chuck he had enough on his plate, Chum and I would handle what we seen as an easy job. Back at the farm the two kids were very excited to see us. Mom said they were okay for a couple of days and kept asking where we were. They weren't there boisterous selves. Mom couldn't get over how their spirits boosted we got home. Riding on the horses one of their big concerns. Jan and Bess took them out. Laura Lee came over to me tugging on my pant leg urging me to take her. Jan laughed and said Bird you always give her a wild ride and she can't get enough of it. Chad looked a little downcast at first also I would also give him a ride. Jan and Bess had the horses settled and ready to go. We had devised a different saddle so we could put the kids in front of us. Work out quite well, made it much easier didn't have to carry them and they enjoyed the ride much more.

Chum and I got busy at the mill making up cedar pipe to carry the water from the spring to the house. Winter the pipes could freeze so we had set up to let the water run through the pipes all winter. The design we came up with work very well we would incorporate the same style at Jan's father's home. We had everything made up and just had to haul it to the city. Henry said he would be the envy of all of his friends. He also took me aside and told me some of the men were really upset about my talk about the Indians. My comment was I was just telling the truth, they just couldn't seem to put themselves in the Indians place. How they would act if things were reversed. Henry just told me to try to hold back. Henry said the bankers and other men as Guys father relied on a lot of these men for their business. They had agreed I was truthful but if they were to acknowledge this they would lose considerable business. I could now understand why they had and commented on what I was saying. Just decided not to go to anymore their dinners. A lot easier to not go save a lot of arguments and probably some hard feelings. Henry's help were good company anyway. The help Henry hired were investigated also his help let him know to hire or not. Chum and I helped in the work we weren't afraid to get our hands dirty. This surprise the help they assumed we would just be standing and watching. We end up with very good rapport with a working group. We also took regular breaks for drink of water a quick snack. This they said no one had ever done wherever they had worked before. I just commented we were workers just like them, they got a big laugh out of this. Work went well finished up with just minor things to take care of in the house. The kitchen help couldn't believe they had running water in the kitchen. Chum had accepted some of the dinner invites and was question why I had not come. He just shrugged his shoulders. Wasn't about to get into any discussion that would lead him into reasons for my not showing up. Chum told me a lot of the men miss my company. I knew there were a few were radicals when it came to being against the Indians. One of the men told Chum he knew I was right. The news media just weren't about to take the Indian side in any dispute. We had finished our work and headed back to the farm, all the news I was hearing wasn't in favor of the Indians. I was upset about how things were going for them, talked about it with Jan. Told her I just had to go back West and see if I could help. Jan wasn't in favor of me going but knew I would never be happy unless I tried. Jan asked if I was going to take anyone with me. I said will be a lot safer for me to travel alone. I would travel away from the main travel trails. Hope I would be able to talk to the Indian chiefs, would talk to them about not signing any new treaties. To try to get the Army to enforce treaties that were already in place. Left with two of my ponies, both were my mares. Now had the one male I had rode out West before his brother had been killed. Traveled leisurely Watched my back trail. Traveled more than two weeks without encountering anyone. Had heard some different travel noises when I was near the main trail. The noises told me it was some army detail. The noises they made were a lot different than the Indians or regular travelers. I made it a point to evade them. Finally ran into some Indians that recognize me. I asked for the main chief, I want to talk to him or them. They were hunting and had poor luck, game was scarce. They would keep hunting, told them where i had seen sign also had heard army on the trail.

They said the Army had moved into the Black Hills, this didn't sound very good to me. They told me were the last camp was where the Chiefs in this area were staying. Was hoping to find White Cloud their, a few more days travel and located the village. There just wasn't the good feelings I had when entering the village. Some of their young men had been killed by the Army troops. A couple of the subjects were there, we had a talk and I tried to tell him not to sign any treaty. Just tell them to abide by the ones that were already in the existence. They listen but I'd didn't know if they even understood what I was trying to tell him. I decided to move on and try to find some of the higher and more respected chiefs. Working through the territory found most were out on the planes. The Indians I had talked to had met with some of the Army and had told them Brave Hawk had said not to sign any treaty. Was thankful that some of the younger men told me about this. They also told me the Army had sent out to scouts to hunt me down. I was now going to be especially on my guard. If I built a fire it would be a quick one just to cook something and not stay with it once things were cooked. Watching my back trail all the time. Had a feeling they were getting close. I built a fire and left and moved so I could see what was going to happen. Left one blanket rolled up as though I were in it. Also left my mare hobbled out where they could see her. I only had to wait an hour or so. One was coming in on the upper side of my camp the other on the side. My mare snorted and the one closest fired into my bedroll. I then waiting for the other to come in. He came striding in, I shot him and the other man dropped to the ground. He was still an easy view and I shot him also. They both had new rifles and plenty of ammunition. Gather up all their belongings and found their horses ,loaded everything up leaving the two men naked and face down. I was surprised to find one of them an Indian. The next village I would come to would give everything to them. There were some Indians not too far away had heard the shots and were approaching very carefully. I started my chant on killing an enemy so if any were around they would know not to shoot me. I was hoping to find some higher chiefs that would be more influenced by my telling them not to sign any treaty. Four Indians showed up, they joined me in my chant. They told me they had seen these men and had planned on ambushing them. I had beaten them to it. They were looking over the rifles and horses. I told them I would trade all. One had an old musket, I took that from him and handed him one of the rifles. He smiled knowing was going to trade all for very little in return. Ended up giving all their belongings to them being and Arapaho usually got the better of the trade they were all in a very good mood. They asked me if I was going to scalp the men I had killed. No was my answer my spirit told me if I did their spirit would be able to follow me and cause trouble. Scalping was not good. This surprise them telling me that the white man did this all the time. I told them my spirits were all

74

Indian even that though I was born white. They all agreed I was more Indian than a lot of Indians and had a big laugh over this. I traveled with them to their village. The village didn't look very prosperous. They were having a hard time just finding enough to eat. The buffalo had not been seen in quite some time. Dear elk bear were also very hard to find. Was glad to see another party of two coming into the village with two deer. There would be a feast that night. This is when I debated if it was worth my while to travel the planes to get my message out. I just told all the Indians not to sign any treaty. The next day two Indians came into camp tell me that other scouts had found the two I had killed. They had turned and headed back to the army camp. I knew I should have buried him. The buzzers gave them the location, any good scout will investigate a buzzard feed. I knew now would be a hunted man. Decided not much else I could do to help had passed the word. Hope they would listen to it, was going to have to be a lot more careful in my travels now. This is when I decided travel mostly at night. A good tracker would be able to follow me if he was good enough. Most would not believe I would travel at night, most would not. I had excellent night vision and most of the time the nights weren't that dark. I also knew a good tracker would anticipate the direction I was traveling and set up an ambush if possible. About a week or more of traveling had the feeling again someone was following me. I had to use my bow to kill some small game, built a small fire to cook and then moved on. They were traveling on my trail during the day time. I realize when I had left that village should have taken care to hide my trail, should have headed West for a while could have found a good cover for hiding my trail my going ahead of the tribe when they broke up their camp. This would have covered my trail by them walking and riding over my tracks. Then I could have found a good place to cut back. I know had made a mistake now had to figure out how to get out of it. Whoever were following were pretty good trackers. I had stopped after moving where I could observe them and realize they were trying to set up an ambush. They were trying to decide on my most likely trail to travel. They knew now I was traveling at night. There were two routes I might take so they went and set themselves up on the two routes I couldn't believe they had not watched my camp more closely. I was watching them instead of them watching me. Decided would have to take one of them out that night. Still daylight made a big loop then started back looking for where he might think I would be traveling that night. Figured he would be a little careless about finding a place. Was right caught his movement, now had to be extra quiet. Waited to get close enough to take him out. Was was either him or me. And I didn't plan on it being me, knew would have to contend with the other one, would have to worry about that later. Took me a couple of hours to get close enough to see where he was. I picked up a stone and threw it pass him , he stood up with his rifle ready, he never knew what hit him my shot put him down. Another shot rang out, I didn't know that this is a single or not. I didn't think the other one would shoot. He would have come thinking his partner had done me in. Decided would head back to my camp and horse being darn careful to make sure the other man wasn't there to ambush me. When I got to where I could see my horse someone was standing beside my pony. Just came to me it was Gonacheaw. Was astounded couldn't even speak just held my hands up and came up to him. He had a grin at my surprise to see him. He then said not to worry about the other man he had met the same fate as the one I had just done in. I asked if he thought anyone else were following. He had already checked and they were the only two. He said they weren't very smart to be tracking you. My comment was all my thanks went to you for teaching me. His laugh came and he said I was the easiest and the best he had taught. I then said only half as good as you. He then told me these two were the best of the Army trackers. We would bury them face down so wouldn't be found. Then I asked how he had come to be on my trail. He had came by some of the Indians I had talked to. They told him about my killing the two other scouts. They also told him the Army had got word out and sent their best after me. He said he knew the two were very good trackers but they didn't know who they were tracking their mistake was of thinking you would be sleeping during the day. Big mistake for them. We then built a fire I had been fortunate enough the night before had killed a couple of grouse that had roosted in a tree near me. We had an excellent meal of grouse. Then we talked till late, then nodded off for a few hours. We had talked to family, Gonacheaw told me it was getting very hard on the planes, the buffalo were becoming scarce. Finding many rotting carcasses, meat spoiled. He then told me best not come out West. There would be war between the Indians and the Army. Some of the Indians would not hesitate to shoot me. The young bucks had no use now for any white man. I I told Gonacheaw they should not sign away any more of their land. He said the main chiefs were of the same conclusion. He said he was heading back. White cloud's father had died. White Cloud stayed with his people Gonacheaw had brought the old Shaman back to where he had asked to be at rest in his holy Black Hills. This is when he had heard I was in the area. Then he started to track me and found two others doing the same. He knew they didn't have good intentions because they were being so careful but not careful enough I said. I didn't know how to take out the second one. Well you don't have to worry now. Travel by day now. Was now anxious to get home to the farm, tried to do some good but didn't know if it helped or not. Gonacheaw left next morning before he left asked if one of the scouts horses was nearby. He had lost his horse in a skirmish a while back. Well now you have two good looking ponies. He knew I would not claim either. His comment, you always gave things away this is why our people love you and respected you without another word he left. My heart ached for him and his people also mine. I believe he knew that time is running out for him and most of the Indians. Riding daylight to dark and sometimes more was back at the farm. Jan could tell that I had a hard time of it. She didn't ask I just held her with my eyes closed for a long time. I took a deep breath and relaxed. Would tell her Chuck and Chum I knew mom wouldn't want to hear. Just as long as I was back safe was all she cared about. Laura Lee and Chad were on my lap right after supper. Would tell them stories about the Indians never anything gruesome. Most about hunting and trapping also escaping from other bad guys. Jan said how do you come up with some of your stories, well I just use some of my past experiences and do away with a lot of the violence. I was quite down for a while just made up my mind nothing you could do out west. Now four of the Army's scouts and couple of the best were not scouting anymore. Felt they were traitors to their own people I knew I would still stick up for the Indians. I was quite popular for a while with my stories. Now with the news how terrible the Indians were made my blood boil. We were the ones invading their land what would you do if you they were invading your home and land. This had not made me very popular. Jan said bird you have to not speak about it anymore. Someone may be just crazy enough to try and an assassinate you just because of your views. I knew would have to be real careful what I said, not that anyone beat me into any of their anti-Indian rhetoric. Because of the news media wouldn't be able to change anyone's mind anyway. I even change my attire and no longer wore my buckskin clothes. Still carried my knife on my left hip. I had Jan help me design my own style of clothing. No dress suits but just comfortable shirts and pants. Started to wear comfortable boots when working. Went back to my moccasins when on the farm. This is the attire would wear in the city so I wouldn't attract so much attention to Jan and myself and anyone I was with. Started to make more trips into the city. Chum and our water pipes were much in demand. Also some of the more affluent people wanted us to do the installing for them. Chuck and Chum said Bird this will make a good diversion for you to get the Indians off your mind. Chuck and mom Sue Bess and Jan were all for it. Knew I would enjoy the challenges of this type of work. Had to do something to get my mind off the Indians. We had to set our shop up to be able to make more pipe. Would hire men to work in a cedar swamp to cut just cedar for our pipes. We then came up with leaving the pipe square and rounding just the ends to fit together. This saves a lot of time and still do the same job. We had made up jigs so everything turned out exactly for a good fit. We had to hire a couple of teams to do a lot of our work. Chum and I had to stop our hands-on work and just supervise the work to be done. If a problem came up we had to make adjustments and corrections. We still made many dinner invites. They weren't the elaborate affairs just good friends and family. Laura Lee and Chad were now riding their own ponies, they were like twins always together. Jan and I had introduced them to the city quite often. They enjoyed the city and especially the theater and acting. Chum and Sue also took them under their wing both were levelheaded. The city Job's went well for both but were always ready to head back to the farm. We had taught both to hunt and fish. The rifles were the new Winchesters. We had found carbine style, this made the rifles a lot easier to handle. Jan and I would make hunting excursions, we taught them both how to track and be very observant and quiet. Chad and Laura Lee were now getting the hang of tracking. They were amazed at how I could read tracks. Had to tell them about my Indian brothers and how much better at tracking they were. I told him Gonacheaw could track on bare stone. Had to tell him about how Gonacheaw Little Arrow and myself knew some of the other younger boys were following us. How we knew I couldn't answer that we just knew. Gonacheaw said let's just hide our tracks then come back on them and surprise them. We then began to hide our tracks, within the next hundred to 200 feet we had left no tracks. We stopped and peed in one spot. Then covered our tracks from their. We made a large circle and came up behind the four or five boys. They were looking trying to find where we had gone, we caught up to them after making our loop. Stayed out of sight until they all gathered together talking and upset because they had lost our tracks. We just walked up quietly and all three of us just stood there. Then Gonacheaw grunted they all seem to jump. They wanted to know where we had gone. We just told them we were standing right hear and you walked right by us. They just shook their heads, then one of them said with Brave Hawk spirit with you you just walked on-air. Gonacheaw little arrow and myself just looked at each other and then burst out laughing. The boys all believe that this is what had happened I told Chad and Lora lee this was how good Gonacheaw and Little arrow were at hiding their tracks plus also tracking. Gonacheaw always commented I was the only one he was unable to track. Laura Lee was quiet for a few minutes then commented, dad you had to be as good as them or the others would've found your tracks. I just grinned and said they were much better than I was. Chad called me uncle and he also agreed with the Laura Lee. Jan said your dad loves his Indian friends very much he always brags them up not including himself. This hunt went very well we spent three or four days in the woods. We all carried our own gear, I packed some of the heavier things. We just made lean-toes out of pine bows for our night stays. Jan and I had bought compasses for Chad and Laura Lee to use and explain their use. They had a lot of fun using them. When smaller They had wandered into the woods, shaking everyone up. They had been playing in the grain and hay barn, spotted a fox on the edge of the woods and tried to follow it into the woods. I was just back from the city that day. Came home to a lot of turmoil I had asked where they had seen them last. They had been playing in the grain and hay barn. Went and started looking for their sign, wasn't long found where they had entered the woods less than a half hour located them. They were glad to see me and wanted me to find the fox. Told them the Fox didn't want to be found so he had hid himself on them. Jan and I told them not to go into the woods without a grown up with them. When they were older we would teach them about the woods. Jan decided she would have to tell them about the dangers. Then proceeded to tell him about bears. Chad and you Laura Lee would make an easy meal for them. Laura Lee said dad would chase the bear away. Jan said yes but dad was away in the city and had just come home. Just don't go into the woods without grown-ups. They both agreed not to do it again. Jan said Bird those two don't seem to be afraid of anything.

Chum and I found we had started another business in the city. We were overwhelmed with the jobs, we're having a hard time keeping up on the pipe making. They readily agreed we then agreed on a fair price for the pipe fittings. We would furnish the cedar pipe they would make the necessary fittings to fit the pipe. Still had a hard time trying to stop talking about our treatment of the Indians. I brought up the killing of the Buffalo, this was their main source of food. They didn't waste anything. I have seen hundreds of carcasses just rotting. Some would say well there killing our people. My answer was it's their home you would do the same if someone was invading your home and killing off all your food supply. A lot of the treaties were not being signed by the major Indian chiefs who are actually in charge. Some would get very belligerent. Chuck and Chum said bird you have to not talk about this you are making a lot of enemies. Decided from then on would go just to the dinners that was required for our business and just talk business. Would not let anyone goad me into talking about the Indians, this was too much a sore spot for me. Our new business was doing quite well, we were also making improvements on the taps we were using. Mom Sue Jan Bess decided to come into the city for another shopping trip. Chad and Laura Lee were excited about going. They both love the theater as did we all. Chuck Chum and I took care of our business during the day, we had to hire a foreman to run our jobs. We made sure that they treated our men fairly. They still wouldn't put up with a shirkers. We also paid better than most so we ended up with good men. After a week everyone was ready to head back to the farm. I still wore my large knife on my left shoulder when ever I was out of the city and also carried my rifle. Mom Chad Laura Lee with Chuck driving the carriage and our overnight gear in our large carriage. Jan and I were riding out front, Sue and chum were behind us. Jan and I were ahead but in view of everyone. We met a man riding toward this city, he passed us and then turn with a rifle and shot at me. The bullet hit my knife and ricocheted into my left shoulder knocked me off my pony. He then turned and spurred his horse back toward the city passing Chuck and Sue. Chuck in the carriage seeing what happened had one of the new revolvers that he had been shooting target with. As a man rolled by the carriage Chuck shot him off his horse. Jan was on the ground with me I was still out and came around shortly. Knew that I had been shot my left arm was numb. Took me a minute to get my breath back. Sue and chum were also down by my side. Chuck told mom to drive the carriage up to us, he was going to take care of this man. The man was fatally shot and knew it. Chuck wanted to know who would had hired him. He said I know I'm not going to make it so won't need the money he promised me. He then told Chuck who hired him. Chuck wasn't too surprised, this guy was a smooth talker and I had upset some of his spiel about the Indians. He didn't appreciate me contradicting him. Chuck didn't tell me or Chum what he had found out. Chuck decided to take this on himself. He had many good friends who would advise and help him take care of this, man who hired this assassin. Sue and Chum brought my pony back. I stood up and mom made me take my shirt off to check on the wound. My knife had saved my life. Mom and Sue prepared and set up camp right there. Had a fire going and hot water and soap to clean the wound. The bullet had not exited was still in my shoulder. Mom and Sue said it had to come out. The bullet had tumbled after hitting my knife carrying a long groove of my ribs, then entered my shoulder. Mom could feel the bullet, she and Sue debated how to remove it. They finally just made another cut and pulled the bullet out. Then applied the herbal magic. I had bled quite a bit and was just beginning to get the feeling back with the pain. Mom had me take something for the pain. The next morning were on our way. Chuck asked me to stay with mom in the carriage. He would take this man back into the city and report what had happened to the police. He wasn't about to tell him what he knew about who hired this assassin. This would be taken care of by him. Mom and Sue Jan Bess insisted I ride in the carriage with mom Chad and Laura Lee. Chad Laura Lee were to handle the team. I finally agreed knowing could have road my pony okay. The carriage road quite well it had springs it took up most of the jolts. The road was now much better from all the traveling. The big wagons did a lot of repair so they wouldn't be consistently stuck. A few of the bridges had a toll but was reasonable the ride home went quite well. Mom Sue Jan would check on my wound three times a day, washing me down with their herbal remedies. When we got back to the farm started with a fever and was down and out for almost a week. just rambled on about my Indian life and Asking for Jan of course she was at my side constantly. Mom Sue Bess were there also doing everything they could to help me. Finally the fever broke, when I came out of it Jan was laying by my side. Just sat up and was surprise, Jan looked as though she was one that was sick. Went to roll on my left side that didn't go well. This woke Jan up, was looking at her with a big grin on my face. She just started crying, her next, word's was we all thought we were going to lose you. Went to sit up and realize how weak I was. Never had had this feeling before. Was naked under the bed clothes. Jan then laughed saying it was much easier to keep you washed down because of the fever. Surprised now how hungry I was, Jan was out of bed and was out in the kitchen in a heartbeat. She was going to fix me my first morning meal. Our cook said Jan please let me fix both of you breakfast. Jan agreed she went and also brought hot water to bathe me again. What a difference in her appearance in just a short time. It was quite early mom Sue Bess heard the commotion were up and into our room to make sure everything was okay. Chad and Laura Lee came in and Laura Lee seen me awake and setting up in the bed gave me a hug, she had tears in her eyes. Dad just knew you weren't going to die on us. Took me the better part of two weeks to get my strength back. My arm was still very stiff. Mom and Sue had herbal ointment also herbals they had me take. Mom said don't baby your arm keep stretching it out it's the only way you will get the proper motion back. She showed me the bullet it was quite distorted from hitting the knife this is what tore up the muscles in my shoulder. Mom and Sue had sown them with sinew cords from some animal. Was well on the mend. My pony was glad to see me. This was my first ride since being shot. Seemed good to ride. Jan Bess Chad Laura Lee accompanied me, we went to our Lake for a few days. I just wanted to walk in the woods, Jan I want to be alone so she and the kids were to stay at the camp. I just went off into the woods to enjoy the woods noises and the solitude for a few hours. I was quite sure new who had hired the assassin and would work on that one back in the city. Came back to the camp Jan Bess Chad Laura Lee had caught trout were preparing them for supper. Just looked at this family of mine was hard to believe was so fortunate to have this love of all. Mom and Sue were still making clothes for sale in the city. They were very good at this, Bess also had got into the act. Guy came and stayed every second week or so. His father and he were doing quite well at their business endeavors. Was now anxious to get back to the city. Chuck had told Chum about what the assassin had told him before he died. He asked Chum not to tell me. I didn't know this but was quite sure knew who it was. This man was a little too congenial, he was overly friendly. Also knew how he felt about the Indians. When I felt had my strength back decided to go and check with Chuck and chum and how everything was going. Chuck said his side was running smoothly. Chum was glad to have me back, he had more business than he could handle. My help was a relief for him.

The next dinner invite this man i suspected was there. He approached me after the meal saying he had heard I had been shot. Just let him ramble on, he had a gift of gab that was very artificial to me. Finally looked at him and saying your dead man. He turned pale and started to stutter. I just walked away from him. Chuck and chum had seen him talking to me, then seen his reaction when I said something to him. Chuck and Chum asked me what I had said to him get such a reaction. I just told him he was a dead man. Chuck shook his head and said we should have told you he was the one who hired the assassin. Now he will try to get you again. I said I knew it was him some of my lower-class friends informed me. They also told me they would take care of the problem. Chuck and Chum shook their heads saying we had plans also of taking care of the blanket y-blank. He always had a couple of hired men as guards. I said is best we not interfere my men are loyal, where his are hired and can be bought off. They would probably tell the police if question that we hired them. We mingle with others of the guests that evening. We had travel to our dinner invite by carriage, all five of us Jan Sue Chuck Chum and I. Jan and Sue had insisted on coming with us to the city, Jan would not leave my side. She told the others I will try to keep Bird out of trouble. We headed back to the inn. Chuck had acquired pistols for Chum and myself and we were both anxious to try them out. New rifles were also out Winchester. The Henry was a big improvement now the Winchester. Still had use my bow occasionally couldn't use it as yet because of my shoulder. Next morning we we had news the man who had hired the assassin was robbed and killed that night. His two guards were at the party, he had left in such a hurry he had left them behind. What his thoughts were when he left the dinner we will never know. Two days later received a small package from the blacksmith shop again telling me not to open it till I was back on the farm. I could conceal it in my pocket it was that small. The police that investigated wondered why he had left in such a hurry to leave his two guards behind. They question them they had no idea why he had left in such a hurry. They asked most of the party and no one had and answer. He had just grabbed his coat and hat called for his carriage and left. Not too far from his home the robbers had throne a branch to one of the front wheels causing it to overturn. He didn't survive the spill his purse was found empty and his fancy jewelry he usually wore was gone. The horses had been cut loose and released. Chuck chum and I agreed they my friends took care of a problem. Chuck asked, Bird was this some of your friends. I just said will know for sure we get back to the farm. Chuck and Chum grinned knowing years before had my answer when I had got back to the farm. Jan even questioned me if I had any thing to do with what had happened. Told her had no idea it was going to happen. This was the truth. I did have a good idea it was he but wasn't positive until I made my comment to him. Chuck and chum then confirmed it. They were discussing what they were going to do and were just starting to formulate a plan. It was a relief to all we didn't have a hand in his death. I knew my friends had found out and took care of the problem.

Chuck mom and Sue had everything pretty well in hand with the farm and sawmill and are other commodities. Chum and I checked out our waterworks jobs, our foreman and men were doing well. Talking it over with Chuck and Chum why don't we just sell the business under a contract and take a percentage of the earnings. This way we would not be tied down to engineering the jobs which took up a lot of our time. We would have a hand in keeping the books. Our men could neither read nor write. We approach both foreman and they were more than happy, this would give them a big boost in money. Chum and Sue were good at the bookkeeping, this was in my liking. Could do it just didn't like it Chad was coming into the city more often with Guy. He wanted to get him started in learning the business. His grandfather and grandmother were getting on an age. Jan and Bess had not gotten pregnant again. We didn't know why Jan and Bess had expected have more children, they told us they didn't know why either. Laura Lee missed Chad when he was at the city, they were like brother and sister. We're hoping Laura Lee would stay on the farm and learn how to manage and handle a lot of the books of the farm and the sawmill. She was very good at the books and had taken interest in running and learning the routine. Mom and Sue were amazed at how quick she had learned everything. She now wanted to breed horses also had brought a puppy into our home. Laura Lee had the puppy house broken a very short time. He followed her all over. Mom said Bird that puppy acts just like your dog he wanted to be wherever you were. Chad was now staying in the city, we miss Bess and Chad they were family. Jan missed them especially as I did. Jan said Laura Lee is caring a knife all the time, will you teacher the proper use of it. I had already shown her how to use a knife. She had to learn how to protect yourself. She now turned a lot of heads, she was one pretty girl. I didn't use my big knife to show her how to use it for protection. I said try not to let anyone get a hold of you in the first place. Showed her the twist and turns to use. Watching a person's face could usually make out what their next move would be. Laura Lee was very agile and surprisingly strong. I was quite sure she would be able to protect yourself if need be. Our farm had grown considerably. Were employing a lot more help and had made accommodations for them. We moved a lot of farm goods to the city. Our apple orchard producing well. Eventually were also a good commodity for the city trade. Venison was at a premium in the city. The deer population had almost disappeared around the farm. We didn't bother with this trade. Found a lot of hunters were using our land to hunt deer to ship to the city. We began to run them off. If we caught them the second time they forfeited their rifle and anything else they had in their possession. After catching a few and they lost all their possessions. Word got out to stay off our land. We had acquired now over 2000 acres closer to three. Thankfully we didn't have too many trespassers. There was a lot of land other than ours. Mom and

Sue had hired another couple and their son to work on the farm. I usually check them out but this time because of me being shot and down for a while I didn't. Apparently had a son and a younger daughter. The son was in his 20s. The girl was 13 or 14. She always kept her head down. Suspected something wasn't quite right. The man acted congenial but got the impression it was artificial. One of the other woman of the other families had kept an eye on them. She warned Laura Lee that the son was watching her all the time. So Laura Lee was on her garden tried to keep an eye out for him. She had headed into the barn to saddle up her pony to make a trip into town with paper for some of the town people. As she entered the barn this guy grabbed her he had put his hand over her mouth so she couldn't scream. I had showed her how to twist and get her knife out. He had banged her head in this scuffle but Laura Lee had her knife out and stabbed him in the gut then again in the chest. He had let go of her the first stab he looks surprised, she then stab him again in the chest. I had been in the village to check out this family. No one seemed to know anything about them. One of the younger boys told me, the man had offered to sell a girl to his father, his father had just turned away. This was hard for me to believe that a father would sell his daughter. Decided to just keep a close watch on them. We had been out early check in on the fields and the rest of our land for trespassers. Finding everything okay Jan and I headed back to the house for our noon meal. I walked into find Laura Lee with with mom and a compress on her head. Laura Lee proceeded to tell me and Jan what had happened. She said she had banged her head but had managed to get her knife out and use it. She had run back to the house and told mom and Sue what had happened. Just turned and went to the barn, the man's trail was quite obvious. He had headed into the woods not too far into the woods had found him he had bled to death from the second stab wound. Would come back and bury them in the woods. Went to one of the other families to asked if they knew about this new family mom and hired.

One of the younger boys then told me about the son trying to molest the supposedly daughter. The father had gave him a beating tell him if molested her they would not be able to get much money for her. Then realize the young boy in the villager was telling me the truth. Went and told the family to pack up and leave and not to take only what belong to them. I now carried my knife and also one of my new revolvers. Told them if they were to steal anything would hunt them down. Shortly came to the house the man barged in demanding his pay. Big mistake on his part, my knife was out and pressed into his got. Told him not to move or he would be leaving his guts on the ground. Then told the young girl to go into the house now. She looked surprised and scooted by me into the house. The man got upset saying she was his. You don't own anyone your money on this girl was wasted. Mom stepped up with what she figured he had coming for the work he had done. Just backed them out to his cart and his woman motioned him to climb up and leave. He said I'll wait for my son. I told him he had headed into the woods after trying to rape my daughter. I'll catch up to him and he will not be alive when I get done with him. The wife then said I knew he would mess up a good thing. Wasn't about to tell the son was already dead. Mom was talking to this young girl. She said her name was Bell that's all she knew. Also found this man had bought her from her family who were not much better than he was. The son had not molested her because the older man had said soiled products weren't worth anywhere as much money. The son had tried once got a caught and suffered a hell of a beating he never bothered her after that. The man and his woman had A close eye on her so she would not run off. I knew this man wouldn't give up this easy. Sat down and told both girls they weren't to be alone at any time. Until this was resolved. The man and his wife had stop at the Sheriff's office and were informed that I was a deputy sheriff. They tried to lie about the girl being there daughter. Chuck wasn't there but had a good man in charge. He just told him he knew we had bought the girl from her family and he could arrest him for doing that. Next he was told to leave the village. He told them we have hung men for less charges stealing was one of them. He got up on his cart and hit his horse hard the horse took off almost dumping his wife out of the cart. Next day went into the village and found some of the kids I had a good rapport with them and asked them to keep an eye out for this man. He was a bad man so don't approach them. They said they would spread the word and if they saw anything they would let me know. Told them to tell the men at the blacksmith shop. They would send someone out to warn us. My shoulder was healing well was able to use my arm again still couldn't quite pull my bow back yet but would keep trying. Enjoyed hunting with my bow because it was so quiet. Things got back to normal. Laura Lee's black and blues were fading. She was also enjoying the companionship of the young girl Bell. She missed Chad and Bell filled the gap. Bell had no schooling so Sue and Laura Lee proceeded to teach her. She was an avid student learning quickly.

A month or better went by without any problems. Then one morning had a young boy coming to the farm out of breath his pony had been ridden hard. He then told me the man I had asked about to let me know if he showed up. He then told me he went up the city road. Then went into the woods and tied his horse up. Took her rifle and headed to the woods. I knew the woods well and had a good idea of the path he would be using. Deer trail that came into our orchard. Took my rifle and went out with a length of rope and an old jacket. Set up in the woods on that trail. Hung the jacket behind a couple of spruce making sure it was just visible. Went to the other side of the jacket away from the deer trail with the rope tied to the spruce and just waited.. Almost an hour went by two deer came down the trail and a hurry. Knew my adversary would not be too far behind. He came along being very watchful. Stopped and looked around every so often. I waited till he got by me and my set up. I then told him to drop his rifle yanking on the rope moving the jacket he turned and fired at the movement. My shot didn't miss he wouldn't fire another rifle again or try and buy and sell young girls again. Only thing I took was his rifle and ammunition. Also had came with a small shovel would bury them in the woods this would be another one of my secret I had told all the farm help about him going into the woods to keep a lookout for anyone sneaking around hearing rifle shots in the woods was quite common so this wouldn't be questioned. I had buried him and had rode my pony into the orchard. Back to the farm leaving his rifle ammo then went from there into town. Found the kids who had spotted the man I had asked them to watch for. Then asked to show me where he had went into the woods. His horse was still tied just untied him and brought him back to the village. Left at the blacksmith shop telling them when he came back to tell him he had best leave for good. After a couple of weeks, they approach me wanted to know what to do with a horse. He said apparent he is not coming back. Wanted to reimburse the blacksmiths for his care. Told him if he doesn't show up sell a horse take what they had coming, then share with the kids I had asked to keep an eye out for him I had already seen they were well rewarded, this would be another bonus for them one of the blacksmiths that I had worked with had died. The shop was still doing well. The other Smithy just supervised the shop now. He and his woman insisted I have midday meal with them. He said I see you have hung up your buckskin clothse. Found the new were clothes a lot more comfortable. We did a lot of talking back and forth of all the things that it happened. A lot of the older time before headed out West. When it was time for me to go he told me when you brought his horse to the shop I knew he would not be back to get it. He had tried to sell the little girl to some of the men in the village. This told everyone he wasn't a very good person. Then after hearing what had happened on the farm knew he was trouble. We were glad to hear the girl had stayed with you we also heard she was doing very well. As I walked out the door the Smithy's said, with a big smile on his face Bird I knew he would not be back for his horse. I couldn't help but grin also. I just didn't feel bad about this man leaving the world with it by my help. There was no one that came looking for him either, just hope we wouldn't have any more problems. Seemed never looked for trouble it always seem to find me. Chuck and Chum were in the city taking care of our business. Jan had been very upset about the thing that had happened to Laura Lee. She had not questioned me about the son or the man that we had fired. Jan finally asked me, she said she knew I wasn't telling the whole story. Love I said it is taken care of. She said please Bird if you don't tell me I will always worry they will sneak back. I told her Laura Lee had done her attacker in and I had buried him in the woods. His father had tried to sneak into the woods and had shot at what he thought was me. My shot didn't miss so both are out of this world and buried in the woods. His rifle had a number on it so had just destroyed it and left it buried in the woods.

Still was worried about my Indian family and talked about this with Jan. Bird you are only one man and you know how the people feel about Indians because of the way they are portrayed by the stories that reporters are saying. We know better but look what has already happened to you because you stick up for them. You got shot in the back and it was very close to doing you in. Also if you weren't around Laura Lee might not be with us also. You know your protection and teaching us how to protect ourselves more than likely save Laura Laura Lee's life. Also Bell would've had a terrible life it was bad enough as it was. Jan I had thought about going out West again but wouldn't be able to do is heck of a lot. I had already told them not to sign any treaties, they had already signed enough as it was. Couldn't think of anything I could do, I wasn't into politics wouldn't know how to handle this kind of life.

Chuck mom Sue and Chum planed on another get together on the farm. We had been invited to so many dinners when we went to the city, mom said we should have a get together for our friends from the city.

Guy and Bess's parents had been out the last time and thanked us but didn't feel up to making the trip again. Jan's dad was more than happy to come out again. Guy Bess and Chad would be coming, his father would keep an eye on the business while he was away. Jan's father asked if it was okay to bring his cook. We always had a good rapport with her. Jan's dad thought the world of her. She had patch me up from the dual I had been shot in. Poor Bell didn't know how to act. She said she would just stay out of the barn. We all laughed and said Bell you are part of the family now. Mom and Sue were making clothes for her and Laura Lee. They were both beautiful girls. Bell with good food and care was really blossoming out now. We had one of our bankers and his wife coming and others Chuck and Chum new. Guy Bess and Chad would be coming early. Mom Sue Laura Lee Bell were all busy planning and getting things ready. With our new add-on we had a lot more room. Jan and I and Laura Lee and Bell would sleep in the barn. Laura Lee and Chad had done this many times with us. Laura Lee always commented how much she had enjoyed it. When Guy and Bess and Chad showed up we introduce them to our new addition to our family. Bell was still terribly shy, Chad and Laura Lee gave each other a hug. Bell had just stood and backed into the background of all the excitement of our meeting. Chad right away asked Laura Lee about Bell. She went and brought Bell over to include her in a conversation. Laura Lee had a big grin she was the first to realize Chad was smitten with Bell. We had thought Laura Lee may be a little jealous, but realize they acted more like brother and sister. Bell was a lot different from the city girls and very pretty. What a difference Bell just seem to blossom out in the time she was with us almost a year. When we sat down to our meal Chad made it a point to sit next to Bell, Laura Lee on the other side. This is when we realize how smitten Chad was with Bell. We were all getting a charge out of it. My comment was that's the way I felt about Jan. Jan just gave me a slap on the arm and grinned. Mom and Sue treated Chad as our own son mom her grandson he had grown up with us. Sue called Chad to her and mom. She told Chad in no uncertain terms he was to be a gentleman. Chad called mom Graham and Sue aunt Sue. He straightened up and said Graham and Sue I wouldn't be anything but. He said he had a few girlfriends in the city but none so beautiful as Bell. He said he had always been a gentleman even though a couple the girls didn't act very ladylike. Laura Lee said she was glad her brother liked Bell in just a week the get together would begin. The week went by fast. Started to welcome our guests as they came. Our home now could accommodate quite a few.

No problems arose and we had every one settled in...... Our first main meal went well, our cooks and help had out done themselves. We were proud to introduce all to our guests. The conversation was about the farm and our sawmill ,also our equipment So far off what they called the beaten path they were amazed at the way things ran so well. Was thankful no one brought up anything about the Indians. This was a very sore subject for me. Had learned to keep my self in check. Had made enemies because of it, so would not comment on the subject. Now when the subject was brought up would just smile and shrug my shoulders. Jan told me how glad she was that I refrained from any comment' others *made. I knew* the news they were getting was how terrible the Indian were.

we were the ones being terrible. A few understood what the truth was, but darn few. The men all went up to the sawmill and were amazed at the way things were set up. Very well organized was their comment. Laura Lee Bell and Chad were roaming the farm Bell had not seen the entire farm. They were having a good time. In one of our pastures they spotted a cow's down one of our milking cows. They started to go and investigate when Laura Lee spotted a bear, she stopped Bell and Chad saying we had just back away slowly The bear had stood up. Fortunately they were not close enough to create a challenge to the bear Laura Lee told them we will head back and tell dad, a bear has one of our cows down. The men and myself were on the way back from the sawmill. Could see Laura Lee Bell and Chad they all waved at us. Laura Lee motioned for me to come to her. She then told me about the cow and the bear. Told the men had a little chore to take care of, not elaborating. Got to the house motioned to Jan, she knew something was up ad was worried I had had confrontation with some one. Told Jan no I wasn't about to be goaded into confrontation any more. Knew now could not make a dent in the way most thought. Then told her a bear had one of our milk cows down and didn't want to upset anyone. Would take our Henry rifles and take care of the problem bear. She then said I'm going with you. Jan then t old mom and Sue what was happening. Chuck and Chum were still talking with the men. Jan excused herself from the group, saying she had to take care of something. Waited till every one was busy talking, then got our Henry rifles out with ammunition. Laura Lee Bell and Chad also were primed to go with Jan and me. We just ambled out of the house with out making much of a stir. Jan then asked how we were to approach the cow that was down. We won't go to the cow, this will probably provoke the bear into attacking. Would scout around to locate where the bear was laying. May be able to shoot with out the bear attacking us. Laura Lee told me where the bear had been laying when it stood up to watch them. Decided the bear had moved closer to where it had seen the kids standing. I told Jan to stay out in the pasture. Will take my time and check out the edge of the woods. No more than got to the edge of the woods, the bear charged, fired two quick shots the bear was almost to me,. Jan also got off three quick shots ,she had seen the bear rise up and had shot he had dropped on Jan's last shot. All the shots to the chest would have done him in. Jan's last shot was to the neck. This had stopped his charge. This was an exceptionally large bear. He was in good shape a lot of fat. Laura Lee, Bell, Chad, said dad I thought the bear was going to get you. My comment was your m om is to good a shot to let that happen. Jan then commented, Bird you always come up with some thing to take the load off your self. We all laughed and relaxed from the excitement. Would go back to the barn and get help to gut the bear and haul back to the barn. We have to clean up the cow also didn't want anything to go to waste. She was one of our better milkers and had been a gentle cow. Laura Lee Bell and Chad sent to the house to let everyone know what had transpired. They all wanted to know what had happened. Laura Lee then proceeded to tell them what had happened. Also embellishing it some. She said we though the bear was going to get to dad but moms last shot stopped him just before getting to me. Had to turn away to hold myself from laughing. Jan just rolled her eyes and grinned. All wanted to know were the bear was now. Told them the men were bring it to the barn, would also see if the meat from the cow was still good. We found the cow had been chewed up but the meat was not spoiled. She had been killed just after the morning milking. This was the first time we had lost an animal to a predator in a long time.

The get together had went real well everyone enjoyed the stay. We had games and dancing in the evening, also story telling. Let Jan and Bess do the telling of our western adventure, Sue would comment every so often. There were a lot of questions during the telling and a lot afterward. Jan had to relate a number of times her being captured by the buffalo hunters and how I had rescued her. Some had asked did that really happen. Jan Bess and Sue all confirmed the story, also how I had went back and taken all their horses so they would not be able to follow us. I was always a little uncomfortable because some couldn't believe it happened. Then Jan's father spoke up and said they should relate how they captured the man who stole from them. Guys father and Bess also chimed in agreeing. How we did this and the police couldn't. Asked Jan to not talk about this to anyone we didn't want to let anyone know how the street children helped and trusted us. Also, the help from our black smith friends. Thankfully it was late evening and mom stepped in saying it was late everyone will want an early start for the city in the morning. They all agreed.

Morning some were anxious to get back to the city. They loved the farm but the city life was for them.. Jan's father was the last to leave. He had brought his cook and now his main companion. They made an excellent pair. Jan and I were glad to see them together. Like mom, she fussed over Henry, he would act annoyed but we could see how much they cared for each other. Henry announced he was going to ask her to marry. He wanted to know our opinion. Jan said, "Dad, you know you don't have to ask us. We love Kay and we're both very happy for you and Kay". Now Jan said, "When are we going to be invited to your wedding?" Henry called Kay over from talking to mom and Sue. He said to Kay, "Who are we going to ask to our wedding?" Kay was flabbergasted. She just stuttered a little then said, "Henry, this is an odd way to propose but I accept." Mom and Sue had come over and had heard. We all had a big laugh and Henry with a big grin said, "I'm glad you accepted." Kay said, "Let's just have family for our ceremony. We can always have a party later." Henry agreed. Mom said, "Looks like we will be off to the city before too long." Sue said, "Henry, you always enjoy surprising everyone." We all relaxed after all our excitement and were glad all went so well.

Chad left with his family. Bess said, "I would rather be on this farm than in the city, but I need to be by Guy's and Chad's side. They both need me at times for guidance." Chad said his good-byes to Bell and telling her he would like her to be his girlfriend. She agreed. Laura Lee was real happy for them. The bear and what was salvaged from our cow was taken care of. We smoked, cooked, and salted the meat to preserve it. The farm was self sufficient. We need salt mainly. We also pickled a lot of different food items. Jan and I, Laura Lee and Bell headed for our lake cabin for a break and to do some fishing. I was also, with Laura Lee's help, teaching Bell how to handle a knife for protection and to keep it hidden but easily accessible. Bell was good at handling it. She had done a lot of getting meals ready and has used a knife e for this. I was teaching her how to use it if someone was to attack her. Laura Lee then told how she had warded off her attacker. Bell said, "I wondered what had happened to him." Laura Lee turned to me saying, "Dad, you tracked him into the woods. Did you kill him?" I decided to tell her the truth. "I found him not too far in the wood. He was already dead." Laura Lee then said, "I didn't feel bad about that. I know he wouldn't be attacking any more girls." Bell then said he had tried it with her and his father had given him a beating because he wanted to sell her for a good price. Jan and I told Bell if anyone asks you, you always tell them you are our daughter no matter what they say or try to do you always say Jan and I are your mom and dad. The woman was still alive. Both men were dead. I had to relate how he had tried to come through the woods with a rifle to shoot me or anyone he could on the farm. I had intercepted him and out-shot him. He wouldn't be a problem anymore. Laura Lee said, "I'm sure glad you're my father." Bell grinned and said, "Me too," Laura Lee then gave Bell a hug saying, "I'm glad you're my sister." Jan and I decided to do a little paperwork to establish Bell as our daughter. Mom said Sue drew up the birth news putting in in our papers telling when Bell was born. A few villagers may know the difference but would no question our word. Jan and I had anticipated the man's woman may try to cause a problem for us and Bell. All the paperwork was done and forgotten about. We got word from Chuck, Henry and Kay's wedding was going to be in a few weeks. He and Kay wanted us to be there. Mom, Sue, and Jan were looking forward to being at their wedding. We knew that Bess and Guy's parents would be having a big party for Henry and Kay. Also, Laura Lee and Bell were looking forward to the theater acting and how we all had enjoyed the theater. Chuck and Chum were thinking about selling lumber in the city. I suggested on just orders that had a down payment on them, with payment on delivery. Chuck and Chum laughed saying, "Bird, you are right. This is what we had planned. Our hard wood would be at much higher price." We already had sold lumber but not by orders. With the lumber there without the orders and down payment, they were always offering much less than it was worth. So at times our lumber just sat there. It always sold at our price but sat for a while. Storage was expensive. Chuck said he and Chum had found a good spot of land and had made an offer on it. Roofed sheds would be build to accommodate the lumber keeping it out of the weather. Mom said Jan had gotten everything ready for our trek to the city for the wedding. Laura Lee was really excited. She couldn't wait to bring Bell to the theaters to watch the shows. She just loved this acting. Bell had really blossomed out. She was an entirely different girl and it was beautiful to see the change in her.

After I taught her how to protect herself, it seemed to instill a confidence she didn't have before. She just wasn't afraid anymore. Jan and I were pleased for Laura Lee and Bell. They seemed to be giggling and laughing all the time. Bell was now also reading and writing very well. These two girls were true sisters. The trip to the city went off without any problems. Henry and Kay had everything prepared for us. I told Jan, "Life can't get much better for us. Two wonderful daughters and a family that was wonderful." I just couldn't find words to express my feelings. Jan teared up a little and gave me a poke on the arm and then a hell of a hug. The wedding went off without any problems. The next thing was the big party. Bell and Guy's mom and dad had planned for Henry and Kay a lot of good food and orchestra for dancing after our meal. Laura Lee and Bell were the belles of the party. The young men were all trying to be the ones for the girls to notice. I thought it was comical, Jan said to me, "Our daughters are carrying knives." I made believe I didn't know what she was talking about. "Bird you also taught Bell how to handle herself for protection." I just grinned and said, "I know it saved Laura Lee's life. That boy would have killed her to keep her quiet." The dancing was going well. Mom, Sue, Chuck, Chum, Jan, and I were also enjoying the dancing. The girls were also having a good time. I always was very observant of the goings on. Watched one boy, he was very rough with the girls. He would just walk up, grab her by the arm and pull her onto the dance floor. I hoped he wouldn't try this with Bell or Laura Lee. He was eyeing both girls. The boys were all vying for a chance to dance with both. He walked over and grabbed Bell's arm to pull her onto the dance floor. Bell took care of this herself. She pulled her knife and kept it low and had it up against his gut. I could see the surprise on hist face. Don't know what Bell said to him, but he backed off with a surprise on his face. Laura Lee had also seen and was there before I was. Bell just put her knife back in the sheath. No one even knew what had happened. Laura Lee knew and was standing by Bell's side. Bell just grinned and told Laura Lee, "Thanks to dad, knew how to take care of the situation." Bell looked over at me and nodded and grinned. I just nodded back to let them know that I knew what was going on. A couple of the other boys asked what had Bell said to make him back off so quickly. She told them they really didn't want to know. She told me after she told him if he didn't want his guts all over the floor, he had better let go of her arm. A little later his father came by apologizing for his son's behavior. He said, "I kept telling him, you can't keep doing this. You will get yourself in trouble. I don't know what your daughter said to him, but I hope he has learned a lesson. I know your reputation, and don't want him hurt." I said, "My daughter already took care of the situation. Most girls don't enjoy being roughed up. I hope now he understands this." I also added, "My girls are farm girls so they are able to handle themselves quite well." The son had left for a while, then came back quite subdued. He went and talked with his father. He then came over to me and apologized for his actions. I told him, "It's my daughter you should be talking to." He said, "I will. Also found she is not to be pushed around. I was under the impression girls like to be handled a little rough." I then I said, "Very few." and asked, "Who gave you this information is way off." He then went over to Laura Lee and Bell and asked Bell to forgive him. Bell said, "Fine, I won't tolerate being roughed up." He said, "I found out in a hurry. Will carry the mark as a reminder." We found out later that Bell's knife had actually drawn a little blood on his gut. Word would get around she and Laura Lee would tolerate only gentlemen. The partey ended with everyone saying that they had a wonderful time. Later, we had made plans to see some of the plays at the theaters. Henry and Kay had made arrangements so we would have special seating. We all enjoyed the plays. The acting was quite good. Of course, some was much better than others. We still enjoyed all the same. Mom, Sue, Bell and Laura Lee made the rounds of all the clothing stores. Also, the material they wanted, finer wool, linen, and cotton. They all enjoyed sewing. Their dresses were all made by mom and Sue with the girls input. Mom and Sue knew the type of clothes I liked. They were more on the workman's style. Even so, I had a lot of compliments on my dress style. I just told the men I enjoyed comfort more than the stiff style most wore. It wasn't long before we headed home. Bell and Laura Lee had met quite a few other girls from the city and invited a few to the farm. A few of the girls were excited and accepted the invites. The parents had to agree. They came by and asked if we had room and if it was true they were invited. Mom and Sue handled everything. They all had horses of their own. This would be a big adventure for them not actually spending time outside the city before. The trip back to the farm went well without any problem. Bell and Laura Lee proceeded to show the girls the house and the barn. They were surprised at finding running water in the house and barns. Bell and Laura Lee told them Uncle Chum and dad rigged it up a long time ago. They also had business going in the city to do this also. The girls rode their pony's side saddle. The were surprised to see all the family riding the way the men did. Bell and Laura Lee wore pants to ride and shocked a couple of the girls. They soon realized how comfortable it was. Also, could control their pony's much easier. Before they left all were wearing pants. Bell and Laura Lee told the girls they at times slept in the barn. They were all for it. Again, a new experience for them. We could hear them giggling for half the night. They said we will sleep in the barn while we're here if it was alright with us. Mom and Sue agreed saying, "If you enjoy the barn, it's fine with us." Wasn't long before it was time for them to head home. The girls thanked us for inviting them and for how much fun they had. They also said they weren't going back to riding side saddle. They didn't care what anyone said. Had one of our men accompany the girls back to the city.

Bell and Laura Lee fell back into their normal routine. They had shown the girls some of their chores was feeding the hens and gathering the eggs. The girls had a ball doing this. They were all good natured and adventuristic. Things calmed down. I was now spending time at the saw mill. The mill was going real well. Chum and I were thinking of adding another saw. We were always behind on our orders now that we were shipping to the city. Chuck also said it would be a good idea. Was working with our foreman and Chum to decide how to proceed. The one steam engine we were using for the planer had enough power to run both the saw and the planer. We would have to come up with a different set up for the planer and the second saw. Most wanted just rough lumber. The planed lumber was much more expensive. We came up with a second shaft and triple pulleys. The steam engine to run the shaft and the two others to run the mill and planer. The other saw would not be affected. The planer would be shut down for a while. Chuck and Chum would do all the purchasing for what we needed. Pulleys and shafting and bearings. Laura Lee and Bell showed up at the mill telling me two men showed up and said they were here after Bell. I told Bell, "You are my daughter no matter what. Don't ever deny this." She readily agreed. "They will try to say you were never seen until recently. We'll tell them you never wanted to go to the city and stayed, with our help. I had already told Judd and his wife so don't worry, and don't look scared. Just stand up to them like you did with that boy in the city." Bell calmed down then. Got to the farm, the two men were trying to talk to the help, to no avail. The first thing out of their mouths was, "We're here after the girl." I just said, "What are you talking about?" Laura Lee put on a good act as if she was scared. They pointed at her right off. I just said, "My two girls are my own and my wife Jan's. Now what is this all about?" "We're here after the girl that belongs to this woman, and we'll take her now." I said, "Before you make any move, look behind you." Jan was standing with her rifle pointed at the two men. I then said, "I threw this man and woman off our farm. The said they would make trouble for us. Now the sheriff is in the city now and I just happen to be his deputy. You can wait in the town until he's back to talk to him, but neither of my daughters are going anywhere. You can tell this woman, the next time I see her, I will cut her throat." They both said, "We were deputized." My comment was, "You're out of your area and I'm deputized for this area. This woman is a trouble maker as you probably already know. So if either of you try taking either of my daughters, you will be dead men." One man turned to the other and said, "That dammed woman lied to us." They both apologized. Well I said, "It's supper time. Seeing you found out she is a trouble maker, you are welcome to have supper with us." They looked at each other and agreed thanking us. Laura Lee looked at me saying,"Dad I'm glad you were here. I thought these men were going to cart me off." Jan and I did all we could to stop from laughing. Bell just looked her confident self. We had a good meal. The men apologized again. They said, "We can see now why she wanted to steal one of your daughters. They are both beautiful. The woman told us one girl would be awful shy and not very pretty. We can see now she is a liar. Our sheriff is going to be real upset with this woman." Jan and I showed the men the births that were registered in our books. We didn't lie, just didn't put the dates when when they were born to us. Nor did we let on that we had adopted Bell. Chuck, back from the city said he knew this other sheriff. He could be quite hard headed at times and if he did show up, he would handle him. He did show up and Chuck was in the village when he came through asking where our farm was. Chuck intercepted him. He let him know he was out of his jurisdiction. Chuck also told him that the man and woman had come to the farm with a boy and girl looking for work. The boy had assaulted one of our daughters. She had gotten free from him so he went into the woods, knowing she would tell on him. Chuck then said, "Jan and I had told the man the woman they had to leave the farm, and they left with the little girl. Chuck then stated the man and woman also tried to sell the little girl to some of the villagers. No one took them up on it. They probably sold the little girl somewhere else and decided to try to steal one of ours. Then the other sheriff said the woman told him her man had come back looking for his son and never returned. Chuck said," The villagers found his horse by the side of the road heading for the city. The horse had been there for a few days. What happened to the man, know one knew." The woman tried to make trouble for us because we had run them off the farm. Chuck also said, "I am the owner of the farm." The other sheriff said, "The woman is very convincing. I just learned another lesson. Some are very convincing liars." Chuck and this sheriff had a good rapport. They would exchange news to keep up on ones that were crooked. Laura Lee was talking to Jan about becoming an actress. She had fallen in love with the theater. Laura Lee asked Jan to ask me if I would object. Jan said, "Your father will not object if it's what you want, he will be all for it." Jan said, "You can stay with your grandfather. He will be delighted to have you and Bell, if Bell wants to." Bell was really please that she was also included. Laura Lee saying, "You are my sister and I would not force you to be with me. Only if you wanted to." Bell broke down and cried. She said, "Your family treats me like I'm their daughter." Laura Lee said, "Well you are. Make sure you always maintain that you are my sister. Chad will be glad you are coming to the city also." Henry, knowing who to contact, found a teacher for the two girls. Bell also said, "I would love to learn how they can be so convincing."

Henry told me an officer of the army had come asking about me. My comment was, "What the blank do they want?" Henry said they had heard I could speak the Indian language. He had told them I could and didn't elaborate on it anymore. It wasn't long and they showed up again. One was a Captain with a Sargent and a couple of enlisted men. The Lieutenant asking Henry if I was here. Henry told him I was. He would send someone for me. He then told him I would often take a hike in the woods. I had just gotten back. Jan and I had taken a long walk to enjoy the woods just to be together and alone. Jan came with me to meet the Captain. He introduced himself and got right to the point of his being here. He said, "We need interpreters who speak the Indian language. We were told you are fluent with the Indian language." I then asked, "What does this entail?" He said will protect you all the time. We hope you would be willing to go west to help keep things calmed down. Very few can speak their language. Jan looked at me, could tell she really didn't want me to accept. He then said they will give me an officers rank. I told him would not accept any rank or uniform. If I did agree, it would be on a voluntary basis and would leave at any time I felt I needed to. The Lieutenant said, "I will pass the word on to my Commander. Talking it over with Jan, she said, "I know if it would help the Indians, you would go. I know they are having a hard time of it." I said," Just maybe I could help some. Jan said, "I know the last time you went, it was very dangerous. You wouldn't tell me any details, so I know it wasn't good. I just want you to be safe." I would go with you, but you worrying about me all the time, so it's best I stay behind. Jan said I know you are going and I will not stop you. Just come back safe.

Rumors in the city had men dressed in uniform and raiding. Outlying farms and sometimes small villages. I knew Chuck and Chum spent a lot of time in the city. Decided to make plans before leaving for the woman and our workers to be prepared for such an occasion. I told Jan mom Sue and Bell were not stay in the house. These men were known to burn the house during a raid. We made three outpost not far from the house set up so had a good view of the house and the barn. Told the workers, Judd would be in charge of what was to be done. All family had the Henry rifle. We stored actual ammunition in each outpost. Made them as well hidden as possible. Had them practice getting to them without being seen. Had Judd tell the workers why we were doing this. They all understood and were happy that we could see this happening and how we could protect ourselves. Most farmers did not have the foresight to be prepared for such an event. Chuck and Chum were back from the city, seeing what I had planed

There, comment was, we were trying to figure out what we should do. Hearing the rumors in the city. We came home and Bird you have set up things perfectly. We've heard that they do the raiding during the day. They are very bold passing themselves off as military men. They are just very bad man. They seem to enjoy raiding and killing. We all hope rumors are not true. They may be exaggerated, and again maybe not. Best to be prepared. Our farm is off the beaten path, we would be a good target for such a raid. The village has grown a lot larger so they should be safe. Again can't be sure. If these men sense and opportunity they will take it.

My family was not very happy to have me going West again. Word was coming back a lot of trouble with the Indians. Hearing about people being slaughtered and scalped. I knew this was not helping the Indians. They were thought of as savages where ever there was any talk about them going on. I knew they could be violent but if they were moving in on our property and land we would do the same. Maybe could do a little good by going out to translate for them. Knew it wouldn't be long before had to leave, so got myself and ponies ready to go.

Headed to the city and stayed at our usual accommodations. Decided to make a few rounds before leaving. Visiting the blacksmiths all told me watch your back not just from Indians then they just laughed. Jan's dad told me he knew I would be safe and he wished he could go with me also wished me well.

A few days later the Lieutenant and the major both showed up. The major told me I would be paid his rate. I also told them will not take an oath only to my terms. I told him at any time I will be able to leave on my own. This was to be put in writing. I was to have a copy stamped and signed. The major said that would be agreeable. They just needed someone to translate the word. Jan and everyone had suggestions. Chuck also stated don't trust the officers they may not be trustworthy. Took two of my ponies would ride one then switch the packs and ride the other one, so they would be accustomed to the pack. They Both were very spirited so by switching had much better control. Both were broken to the rein, my mare had just sensed my movements on her back and would respond immediately. My ponies were great but never could match my mare. Met up with the Lieutenant and two enlisted men a sergeant and a private. Meeting them felt they would be good companions. The lieutenant was young and inexperienced. I believe that Sgt. was chosen to help guide him. They all seem anxious to get started, a lot more than I was. They had a mule for a pack animal. I was off my pony waiting for the other's to mount. The mule came and nudged me, had to acknowledge him, he was a beautiful animal, we made friends within a few minutes. The two enlisted men looked at me rolling their eyes and nodded at the Lieutenant. We went out just a short ways. The Lieutenant informed me he was going to be in charge. I just answered like hell you are. I turned around and headed back to the post. And the Majors office explain what happened and was not about to take orders of any kind from from the Lieutenant. The major grinned and said I will handle this. He is a little too big for his britches will take the arrogance out to him now. The major then said with a grin you will hear me quite loudly. He then called the Lieutenant in, gave him one hell of a chewing out and threatened to have him court-martial ed. He told Lieutenant I was a major the same rank as he was, if he didn't want this assignment he should not have volunteered.

The two enlisted men were grinning. When the Lieutenant came out he was almost dragging his feet. He walked up to me and came to attention and saluted, he then started to apologize, I just nodded and said if you're going you best mount up. The first night out went buy the rules. One of the men was a good cook, the first meal was surprisingly good. The two men smoke pipes and had a good supply of tobacco. They relaxed and lit up, the Lieut. was by himself, could see very uncomfortable. My next words Lieutenant i want you to join us. You will have to get comfortable with all including the enlisted men. Told him was going to go alone but the major told me you needed the experience, also living with the Indians I had learned the language.

Now out of the city put my knife on my shoulder. Had not done this in quite a while, my arm and shoulder had healed well very little loss of movement. The bullet that had hit my knife left a mark on the blade. The cook seeing me put my knife on my shoulder, he then commented. Blanket y-blank I know better than to pick a fight with you. His comment to the other men was, he killed 12 to 20 men in knife fights. I couldn't help but laugh, just told him everything gets exaggerated. He then said I seen one of your fights with the best knife fighter in our area. He challenge you, you tried to ignore him. We had all our bets on our knife fighter. All thought you were afraid of him. He attacked you, it was over and less time that I could blink lost my bet Someone knew who you were and bet heavy on you. Told them had no intentions of doing him in but he was determined to do me in wasn't going to let that happen.

When things calm down told them we are going to make some changes before we go too much further. We have to get rid of all the rattling and clinking. We are only four if the Indians are riled like I believe they are our hides aren't worth much. Pots and pans must be anchored so they don't rattle also metal on the horses has to be done away with or find a way so that don't click. An Indian can hear this for miles.

They are attuned to nature, any noise made other than naturally they will know. Everyone was quiet for a while, the Lieutenant spoke up asking if I had killed many Indians. No was my answer and only in self-defense. I have many Indian friends. We are invading their land. None of you would be very happy with someone was taking your land and forcing you out. The cook spoke up saying you didn't kill many Indians but you made up for doing a lot of men in in the city. I said again only in self-defense. All was going well Lieutenant was fitting in well. He told me he had made the mistake of thinking I was a buffoon because of my buckskin clothes.

I was again using my bow with a lot of practice was back up to my original accuracy. After 8 days out I stopped our group then told them we would be meeting some Calvary soon. They just shrugged their shoulders and had a smirk like on their face. Three or four hours later they showed up on the trail. A captain leading this detail, I let the lieutenant do the talking. The captain had asked what we were doing so small a group. The lieutenant told him they were on escort for myself. I was fluent in an Indian language. The captain stated you are looking for the major at one of the post. He also told the lieutenant to head back as soon as he and his men could. The major was not very trustworthy. The lieutenant said he had his orders to head back. The captain said he will order you and your men to stay, just be careful.

After hearing this I knew would release the lieutenant and men before we got to the post. Lieutenant was learning from me how to approach different parts of the trail so we weren't ambushed. His statement to me was how glad he was to have such an experienced leader. After the Calvary were on their way again all want to know how the blanket y-blank did I know we would be meeting the detachment, more than half a day ahead of time. I just laughed and said some secret I will not divulge the two enlisted men just shook their heads stating glad were with you. Had everyone stop early had seen grouse sign that was fresh. Would try to get a few for our evening meal. Went with my bow, told the Lieutenant to just stay behind me. The noise we made would alert them. They would fly when and if we got close. Was ready and downed one as it took flight, the second one was up and going and I down that one also. On the way back to our bivouac downed the third. We entered the camp the cook had a fire going and was delighted to see we had three grouse. This would last a few days, the lieutenant said to the men he got all three on the wing. I would not want Bird shooting at me with that bow. A few days later had them leave the trail and be quiet.

They now didn't question what I asked him to do. Had sensed Indians and didn't want to have a problem. I would face them first and tell them what I was up to. There are eight in this group. Surprise me they didn't know I was at the side of the trail waiting for them. I just rode out to let them know I was there, I couldn't get over there surprise. I had my rifle out and crossed in front of me. I could tell a couple the younger ones weren't happy at seeing me. All of a sudden the older one leading the group hollered Brave Hawk. He rode right up to me, I did recognize him, he was the one who shot arrows at me and I had been fortunate enough to deflect both. Had made friends with him quite a while back, we both held each other's shoulders. His comment was you haven't gone to the big spirit, all I said was you haven't either. We both had a good laugh at this, he turned to his group and told him I was Arapaho, many had tried to kill me but all were at the happy hunting ground. The rest excepted me, except for the two younger men. Just hope my group would stay put. Then told them what I was doing, this major needed someone who could speak Indian. They told me they were on their way to a trading post, they had pelts to trade being early we parted, I went on my way they headed down the trail also.

Had a bad feeling about the two younger Braves could tell they had been watching me. As I rode, the sense I was being followed was very strong. rode a ways further and found a good spot to observe who was following. Figured they would be a lot quieter, but waited till they passed me, they sure were very poor trackers they should have seen where I had left the trail. Then rode up behind them could tell they were startled. My rifle was ready just prayed I would not have to use it. One snapped his rifle up I was ready his rifle went off as he hit the ground........ The other just dropped to his knees and started his death chant. I then spoke to him asking why they wanted to kill another Indian. When he realized I wasn't going to shoot him he calm down. He said his friend had thought I would be an easy kill and we would have a good rifle. Told him to get his horses and load him up and join his group. Tell them Brave Hawk can't be killed by an Indian.

Went back to where had left the lieutenant and the enlisted men. Lieutenant was upset heard the shots and thought they had got me. The lieutenant said one of the men was going to light his pipe and he stopped him. You understood what I had told you the Indians would have picked up that smell and would have come looking for you. all want to know what had happened, told them had met friend's and had a good talk. As we parted watch two younger Braves lag behind the group. My feelings told me they were up to kill me and rob me. The two had also dismounted and were jogging on foot following me. As they went by stepped out behind them asking if they were looking for me. One snapped his rifle up, my bullet hit him in the chest he went down with his rifle firing into the ground. The other didn't try anything, let him go to tell the others what had happened.

They then asked if the group would be coming back to get me, I answered no it was the two young Braves idea and not the groups. So not to worry about them. Most know me and wouldn't think of trying to kill me. We were on our way again this trail was well used by both Indians and people and Army. I told the lieutenant would release him before we were to meet this major. The lieutenant didn't know what to say, told him the impression was that he would order you and men to stay at that post. Would tell him I release you days before. Now I also gave you enough pointers to keep you safe on your way back. Your major is a good man. I will sign your orders as a major. He also knew I would take orders from no one. We had no other problems.

Told the men there's an army patrol I could hear them. I am going to release you and the men now. Stay hidden till I ride off with this patrol, then head back and ride steady and kept a good look out and always stop on the downwind side of the trail.

Waited for the patrol they were coming down the same trail we were using. A lieutenant was leading them. When the lieutenant spotted me he halted his men. Just rode up to him telling was looking for this major. Lieutenant said he is my officer in command. He then asked me what my business was, told him was an Indian language interpreter's, sent out by the Army to interpret for them. Was glad I had the official Army paper stating I held the rank of major. When he looked at the paper he came to attention and saluted told him this is not necessary, when in Indian territory you and I would be the first ones to be done in if they could. The lieutenant said my major would have us in the stockade for not saluting. All I said was oh shit. The group over heard me and laughed real hard. I had the feeling would not get along very well with him.. Told the group to head back and I would catch up shortly.

On loaded all the provisions from my pack pony and gave them to the lieutenant and men, told them if they were careful they should have enough to get them back. I knew alone I could live off the land.

We shook hands as I was ready to leave the LIEUTENANT asked if he could salute me I readily agreed and returned his salute.

The men told me they were very surprised how being a major didn't enforce any discipline. My answer was with men like you wasn't necessary.

Then was on my way to catch up to the patrol, when I did the Lieutenant asked if I would join him up front. No would stay behind was more comfortable in the rear, he nodded and went back to the front. Shortly we rode into the post, the lieutenant went in to report. He came out in a hurry saluting me saying the major wants to see you -immediately. Took my time checked on my ponies releasing the pack on my pony used for the trip. As was finishing up a sergeant came hurrying up saying the major wants to see you now. Thank him and kept doing what needed to be done. Then went into the post headquarters, was surprised at how fancy it was for outpost. The major, could see he was upset. The first thing he said to me where's the rest of your men. Played dumb asked him what he was talking about. The men that came with you I know you didn't come alone. I said release them a few days back they were on their way back 'being in buckskin he thought I had no authority. He said could have used them here you had no right to release them. Was prepared took my papers out showing him was also a major. He read them looked at me and started to put them in his desk. Just motioned to hand them back to me, he he hesitated but knew by the look on my face would forcibly take them back. Put them back in my pouch and had better keep them on me all the time. His next words were I give the orders here. My answer was to your men but not to me, and here to interpret the language. Then asked where your scout's are. He said they stay outside the post. Turned to leave he said I didn't release you yet. Pulled my knife off my shoulder and wrap the point on his fancy desk made sure left a good chip out of it. Told him it was enough of his nonsense I also hold the rank of major and you will not give me orders

113

I'm not here to lick your boots. Could see his two orderlies were scared out of their wits. Now do we have an understanding he nodded and I left quite upset, not as shook up as he and his orderlies were. Went back to my ponies asking where the Indian guides were. The lieutenant had one of his men show me where the scouts stayed. Went over to greet them, one turned his back the other one looked me over saying you are the new interpreter for the Army. He then stepped up and said we will be friends putting his hands on my shoulder and me on his. We began to talk, the other Indian left he nodded toward him, his comment surprised me he said will have to kill him one day and laughed. We visited back and forth he finally asked if I was out to help the Army. Look at him and said really here to see if I can help my Indian brothers. You call us brothers? Yes I am an Arapaho he then looked at me again saying who was Gonacheaw? He could see I was kind of surprised. He's my brother who taught me to track. He then was surprised saying now I know you your Brave Hawk. Acknowledge this with a smile. He said was there when you attacked the grizzly and killed him with your knife. We still laugh about the brave underneath the grizzly chewing on his rifle and not being harmed couldn't help but grin saying a lot gets exaggerated. His big smile and said not that time was there. decided to ask about the other guide. He is not good he sides with the major is a badger ,at times talks with a forked tongue. My comment will have to be careful in interpreting for them the other guide came back in the tepee and got something and went back out, I will kill him soon the other guide said.

Was set up just outside will not stay on the post, telling my new Indian friend had had bad words with the major already. Lieutenant had passed the word was also a major. They were surprised I was wearing any resemblance of a uniform we the guides were to be sent out to talk to the Indian chiefs they were mostly locals. Chiefs but not that much authority especially to make any kind of treaty. The way the major talk would get them to sign some of their land away for nothing more than trinkets. Most didn't even realize what this meant. They thought they were gifts.

Proceeded to let them know the major was speaking with a forked tongue. When telling the Indian chiefs this. The other guide that would not stay in the same tent we stayed in, could tell he wasn't happy what I was telling them. Told them to accept the trinkets, but refused to agree to any terms the major put forth. We traveled quite a lot to find different tribes and chiefs. The one Indian guide continued to ignore me and the other guide. We decided to head back to the Army post and tell the major that

there would be Indian chiefs showing up before too long. My new friend and I went out on a hunt when we got back to the post we told them we had seen bear sign a few miles from the post. This would make a big change from the food at the post. Used my bow to hunt birds my friend and myself enjoyed our own cooking. The birds were delicious, we both know about wild herbs to add to the flavor. The major sent for me asking when the Indians would show up, all I can tell him was they live by their own time and could tell him by the end of the new moon, they would probably show up. The major said why didn't you insist they come in right away. I said I told them this. They told me to tell a major that they weren't tied to time like we were. Could tell he was upset with what he heard from me. My new friend agreed with me, the other Indian guide just stood stone-faced with no comment. A couple of weeks and the Indians started to filter in setting up tepees. My friend and myself greeted them. The other guide stayed aloof from us and the Indians coming in. The major came to see the Indians setting up, could tell he was pleased to see them. I knew he was hoping to get them to sign with a mark to agree to the trade for their land. Shortly the Major Sent the captain to tell me he wanted see me and the guides the one guide went right away. My new friend and I were visiting with some of the Indians that we had not met they said they were here to receive gifts from the soldiers. The guide that we didn't like had also been talking to a lot of the Indians we had not met in our excursions. My friend and myself are not happy he had told them they were gifts. We both know they were a trade item. Finally we decided to go see the major. We could tell he was upset with us for not showing up when he sent for us. He was quite belligerent telling us he had sent for us that morning. I answered by saying well were here now what was so important we had to jump at your beckoning. He then kind of blustered out I want to start a meeting with the Chiefs. They aren't settled down as yet. They have their own time agenda and I can't change it. Finally he seem to realize I or the Indians weren't going to be bullied into his commands. The men he controlled suffered under his command. He changed his attitude and became congenial asking me to let him know when they were ready to meet with him. Took a couple of days before the Indians settled down and decided to meet with the major. One Chief we had met before he was more or less in command of the of the lesser Chief's, no they would not understand what was going on if and when the major wanted them to sign away their land for the so-called gifts. The major had his men set up tables with blankets and a lot of beads and trinkets quite impressive to the Indians they were invited to look everything over. When the chief settled down the major called to me went over to find out what he wanted me to tell the Indians. He said to tell them all this was theirs if they would first just put their mark on the papers they had ready for them. I knew he had no knowledge of the Indian language, told the Chiefs that the major said they were gifts but he speaks with a forked tongue. When you make the mark on the paper you are giving your land away to him for the blankets and trinkets. He would use the soldiers to keep all Indians off of the land you made your mark on. The Chiefs then went into a confab. Then heard the main chief tell the others if they made a mark on the paper he would kill them. Some had wanted to take the blankets and trinkets and not truly understanding what was meant by their mark on the paper. The major thought everything was going well. One of the main chief stepped up to the table and proceeded to pick up the goods and throw them down on the ground. That evening all were gone was afraid the major may order his men to attack the Indians. The major was so startled by all that happened all he could do but keep asking what had happened. I went with the Chiefs telling them they had made the right decisions could tell the lesser chiefs were not happy about it. They just knew they were not going to get any of the so-called gifts. The main chief who I had known before knew what was happening to his people. My new friend and the other guide traveling with the Indians for a while.

Returned to the post, went to our camp for the night and found some of my clothing missing. None of my other belongings were touched. This left me wondering what anyone would want with some of my clothing and not take things of more value. Just thought hope they enjoy wearing my clothes. Knew the major would be real upset if he found out what I had told the Chiefs. Next morning the captain came when I was bathing, to tell me the major would like to see me. The captain said be careful he is real upset. Finished my bathing and then went to see the major. He was sitting at his desk my guide friend standing next to him with a stolid face. The major welcome me and said one of my guides I have sent out to try to change what you told the Indian chiefs, he then raised his hand from under the desk holding a pistol he then said my other guide said you told the Indians I was speaking with a forked tongue which meant I was lying to them. My comment was told them the truth. He then said I'm going to kill you for that. My friend grabbed his hand holding the pistol he also stopped it from firing his next move was a knife to the major throat the major rollback blood gushing from his mouth as he tried to holler, but just blood and a gurgle what was all that came out. My friend then said I have returned the debt that my brother owed you for killing the grizzly bear before it could kill him. He then told me the other guide is dead with your clothes on him. He had been scalped and disfigured to look like you, we will leave with you in front of me so will seem I am taking you prisoner they will think I killed you. We will leave together, your horse and belongs are where I killed the other guide for not being true. We got to where the other guide was laying, being scalped and mutilated they would be sure it was me he had killed. The Army wouldn't come looking for me. We could hear a lot of commotion at the post they must've found the major with his throat cut. Time for us to leave we took a trail my guide knew about anyone following would have a hard time not knowing the lay of the land. We traveled night and day for five days then checked our back I knew so far no one was following us told my friend this. This his next comment was Gonacheaw taught you well I then said I will travel with you to meet Gonacheaw. He then said no we would separate. Gonacheaw told him I wasn't to go back, would do more good back the white man's place.

He also told me the two chiefs that wanted the goods the major was offering were very upset with me. They would know you weren't killed by me they also think you killed the other guide they had two or three maybe more watching the outpost. We may have fooled the soldiers but not the Indians those two chiefs will send their best trackers after you. We travel fast enough to be a head of them for a while when we parted he said we are now brothers just nodded in agreement. Could not have asked for a better compliment.

Some of the lesser chiefs just couldn't see the big picture what was going on. The buffalo were being killed at an alarming pace. He also said they know you have a rifle with many shots so they will be extra careful in approaching you. They will try to ambush you so watch for this. Try not to follow the main trails. A lot of our younger men will feel it is a great honor for them to kill Brave Hawk.

Some of the ones who will be following you are good, but will find they aren't good enough. Quite a few have tried word has it you have a great protection and no Indian could kill you. A white man may be able to. Would have liked to travel with him but his advice was sound. Could picture a lot of hardship for my Indian brothers.

Decided to travel very leisurely much easier for me to sense any following or any trying to setup an ambush. Less than three days knew was being followed. Decided to see how many were following. Watch for a good hill That I could watch from, rode to the top turned back to the back of the hill, turned and went back down and up the trail again. Made a large loop back to the top of the hill to watch my back trail. The impression was giving them was that I camped on the hill then had continued on, and a few hours they showed up. One seem to be leading. Five are in the group, the leader was older than the other four. Knew he would be the most dangerous one, let them pass and continued back down behind them, was hoping this would discourage them from following me. They would now know I knew they were following me. Turn off the main trail and onto a to a deer and elk trail, by doing this I would make it very hard for them to set up an ambush. They would have to know the lay of the land and know how the elk and deer would act also. This trail led me to a small valley that had water and good feed for elk and deer. Then decided would be a good spot to confront them. Went through the brush and took my pony's at a distance and left them to graze. Went back down to the trail to the edge of the Valley wasn't long when three showed up with one acting as leader in front. When I spoke and showed myself he dove off his pony into the brush. The other two threw their rifles up to shoot. Was prepared had a lot more practice than they, shot both off their ponies only one was able to get a shot off. The leader was on the ground and was well hidden by the brush, turned and left back to my ponies. Knew the other two would've heard the shooting and headed for it. The leader now also knew how dangerous it was to be following me. Hope they would now give up and go back.

Would also have to be a lot more cautious myself if they continued to try for my hide. Went back to my ponies and made a loop around them to make sure no one was there, my ponies weren't upset so knew no one was around. Was when they came trotting to me. Decided to run alongside and in front of my ponies needed this for relaxation, did this for a couple of miles found a good spot to have a meal and let the ponies browse. Could sense they had not given up on trying to kill me. They would probably have lost face. Waited till almost dark then took both my bow and rifle started back on foot to locate them could smell smoke wasn't sure if it was white men or the ones that were following. Took my time approaching in the dark. It was three out of the five sitting by the fire having their meal discussing what to do next. The one was saying he could and should have killed me when he had met me but his pony had dumped him off. He would kill me the next time he met me. I then step up and said I'm here, he went for his rifle my arrow went through his chest he turned as if surprised and fell to the ground on top of his rifle. The other two just froze in place, both started chanting this was a death chant. I stepped out to tell them if they would now turn back their life would be spared. Both calm down, then asked why they were trying to kill me. They said the Chiefs had sent them because I had spoiled their getting all those gifts. Then told them they weren't gifts they were to trade for their land. The Chiefs has said I would be easy to kill because I was a white man. They also told me another older Indian had said we would be all killed he knew who I was and had encountered me and Gonacheaw before and was fortunate to survive. The younger men then told me they had just laughed, the one that was leading them was their best tracker and bragged he would be the one to kill me, no white man was as good as he was. They then told me also that there was a father and son from the other tribe that were following me he was away better tracker than the one that I just killed I then told them to to bury him face down and go back and help their people.

We will and the chief will be shamed and have to leave. Now knowing there was but two more after my hide. Would be very careful and watching for an ambush. Was warned that the older Indian was their best tracker and sent by the other chief. Had carried both "'my rifle and bow" but by not using my rifle the other pair would not be alerted that something had happened. Headed back to where had set up camp took a long time for me to get there, circle my camp very carefully used what Gonacheaw had taught me he called this the hidden from your enemies, you sent out your thoughts to anyone following trying to ambush. When he first did this was very skeptical. He proved this worked on other occasions, now did the same thing with this last two. They would set up a cold camp with no fire to keep themselves hidden they didn't know had been warned by the other two young Braves. After making my circle around my camp and ponies felt they were not close as yet. So built a fire and cooked a grouse had killed with my bow a few days before. Would set up my own ambush for them. Could tell they were being very cautious. Could feel them getting close, then would sense they backed off. This told me would have to be extra careful where and how I rode. Stayed off the main trails and followed elk and deer trails, would break off the trails and make my own way heading east. They had set up a couple times to ambush me, just sensed this and had made a leisurely detour making them think they were just having poor luck with their set up. This went on for a few days, then decided would make a day camp with fire and all to give them the impression that was now not being hunted. Laid things out as though would be spending the day and night., Had made a special sling for my rifle. This was a rifle with a much shorter barrel and was quite easy to carry and still use by bow. Never had to hobble my ponies they always came on my whistle. Had trained them from very young. A stranger would not be able to get close enough to catch them. Now could sense were close but not close enough to get a shot moved away from my camp set up tried to give the impression was going on a hunt for bird or rabbit. Once I was out of what knew was their vision made a fast loop back to the area where they would set up they may or may not have figured I did this on purpose. My ploy worked quite well even watch where they set up in some brush for their concealment. At dusk decided to move in on the older Indian, watched him constantly he had set up in some brush for concealment. Knowing where he was made it easier to get close enough to get a bow shot off. Was moving in facing him, had crawled on my belly for over an hour. Rolled on my back and got my bow ready. He had no sense was that close to him, when he looked away from my position got up and loose my arrow. The arrow hit him in the chest, he had turned ,had aim at his heart. Heard him grown as the arrow hit him knew had not hit where had aimed. Moved in a hurry from where I had let the arrow loose to a slight depression that I had used to get close to him. Then heard him say quite loud, Brave Hawk you have killed me but don't kill my son. He then said my rifle will not be pointed at you. Moved closer staying out of sight. His son may be moving to find what is now going on. The older Indian then called to his son to come to him. Watched his son, his rifle on the ready, he was told by his father to put his rifle down. The son hesitated but then the lowered and uncocked his rifle, the old man said it's true Brave Hawk can't be killed by an Indian. I then spoke up telling them to put their rifles aside and would come to them. The father then said son put both are rifles up against that tree. The son did as told. Moved in and checked on the Indian with the arrow through his chest. He was very fortunate the arrow had not hit heart or lung. Would break the arrow and pull it back out of his chest. He didn't even flinch, some blood but not excessive. Then told him he would be okay. His next comment was you gave me and my son our lives.

I told my son really believed Brave Hawk knows where we are all the time. My son didn't believe a white man would be that good. Then Asked them if they knew Gonacheaw they both said he was the best tracker they knew. Then told them we were brothers he had taught me well.

The son then asked why had not killed them. Told them Indians are my brothers would not harm any only when they are trying to kill me. Went about fixing the meal for the three of us. The son as we were eating said no one believed the stories they have told about you. Then he asked did you know all along we were following you. Then told them about the three times they had tried to ambush me, knew you were there and would find another trail. Father said he knew that you knew. I didn't believe him I do now. Told them was hoping you would give up following me.

The next morning gathered herbs to help heal the wounds on his chest told him he should walk and not ride for a few days, had a leisurely meal and started to pack up. The son then asked could we become blood brothers. Felt this was a nice compliment, usually a Shaman was involved to have the spirits connect with the ceremony. We knew if all were willing it would happen the father then spoke up saying Brave Hawk will not want us for brother. My answer was I consider you as brothers now. We will be blood brothers if your father is willing, this brought a large smile to his face. A nick on the left wrist and then holding arms for a while or so and it was done. They would later have it sanctioned by their shaman. Before we parted had to ask if any more were following. Both said the other group and they were the only ones they knew were following me. Headed down the stream wanted to clean up the wounds I had created. Packed with herbs look good no blood and no coughing. Decided to bathe before leaving, the son said to me now see why your called Brave Hawk. The Scars on my chest and back and arm, he then said you have survived many trials, this was told to me before didn't try to elaborate they would believe what they wanted. Before parting again said don't ride for many days to let your chest heal I'm now happy my arrow was not accurate.

The older Indian said the spirits wanted it to happen. Told them to also tell all was going to do my best to help the Indians. Then told him the white man use paper to spread the word to all white men they also called Indian savages. Told them the buffalo hides were sent across the big waters to other white men. Father then said they were like leaves many are coming into our land a lot are coming and digging next to our streams looking for yellow metal. They could not understand why this was so precious to the white man. All I could say they use this as a trade as you use pelts as a trade item. Now that I knew no other Indians will be following. We parted as brothers with hands to shoulders and a nod.

Took my time stopped at a small lake making sure no one was around went in first the lake was cold but invigorating. Stayed for a few days reminiscing of my time with running deer was one of the happiest times in my life. How fortunate to now have a family, wife and daughter, how fortunes have changed. Decided not to waste anymore time and proceed to head home to the farm. Less than a week was at the boat landing the young man there didn't recognize me. Had not bothered to take any coin with me out west he wasn't going to let me on the ferry, just nodded and started my ponies to the river. Then heard a holler to wait, the man knew me he was actually the one who knew me well as Bird. He was all apologize his grandson was quite new to the job. He then told the boy, Bird crosses any time without charge. He looked at me and kind of shook his head saying they are going to be surprised to see you. After crossing met a few that I knew, they looked at me kind of stunned then just waved. Arrived at the farm close to dinnertime, all seem to be stunned to see me.

Next came a heck of a yell Laura Lee came running and jumped into my arms dad dad we were told you were killed by the Indians. Didn't expect this or would have not wasted so much time enjoying the country knowing would not be traveling it again for some time.

Laura Lee began to cry, mom is in the city with grand father and Bell. Next question was what happened what happened. Long story Laura Lee will relate later. Will get cleaned up and head for the city. Laura Lee said I'm going to saddle my pony. Just hollered Laura Lee please wait for me , got to get cleaned up and changed. Wont be that long and we will go together.

Stopped only to eat and let the ponies browse. We had also brought grain to feed them. Four days and the fourth morning we were in the city. When we got to Laura Lee's and my father-in-law's house she was off her pony and into the house before I could restrain her. Being early morning breakfast had not been ready. They were just starting the cooking. My father-in-law's grooms were all surprised to see me. They just told me we will take care of everything just go to the house. Laura Lee was trying to tell everyone at once. Jan was just coming down the stairs Laura Lee said mom you have have to sit down. This is when I came into the room, Jan turned pale I thought she was going to pass out. She recovered and we came together with a smothering hug. All Jan could say, Oh Bird what happened the major said you were killed and the other major also. Bell saw me and started to cry. Laura Lee went over to her and gave her a hug. Mom and aunt Sue heard the commotion and also came down to the stairs. Mom just smiled and nodded, Sue had to come and give me and Jan a big hug. Mom then came over and gave me a hug. She then said I told them you would be home. Chuck and Chum were out taking care of some of our enterprises. We all finally sat down for breakfast. The cook and maids jaws dropped in seeing me they had been told I was killed. A little later in the day Chuck and Chum showed up for lunch. When coming in they knew something was happening every was in a good mood smiled and just were exuberant. Mom and Sue both started to talk at the same time. Then they both laughed, mom then told them, Bird is back he wasn't injured or killed. Chuck and Chum both said was darn hard to for us to believe he had been killed, Bird has too much experience and know-how to avoid most any challenge. They wanted to know where I was. Mom told them Jan and Bird went for a walk up in the orchard. They should be back anytime now. Shortly Jan and I came into the house by the kitchen. Everyone had just sat down for a snack and tea. Chum got up and came over and gave me a bear hug. Chuck also came over putting his hand on my shoulder saying we were hard-pressed to believe you had been killed. With your experience would have been a piece of very bad luck. Now we are all anxious to hear what happened. With the kitchen help I wasn't about to tell what had actually happened to the major. Then said will tell all at our dinner party. Even Jan's father Henry, said he wasn't sure was waiting to hear more from the major who had personally come to inform everyone that bad news. Knew for the first time would have to make up a falsehood of what had happened.

All wanted to know what had happened. Told every one would relate what had taken place later. Later got just the family together to tell them the truth but would tell the Army a different story. Let just the family know what had actually happened. Would later relate my whole experience and why I was so long in getting back. Told the family would tell the major I had left because the other major insisted I would lie to the Indians so packed up and found some of my clothing missing. Both guides weren't there either I knew that the guides were not on good terms. One of the guides disliked me and would not share the other guide and my quarters. What happened after I left was news to me. Told the family that because the other guide had cut the major's throat and me with my knife on my shoulder would be the one they would blame for his death. All agreed to relate the story to the Army so would not be surprised also would tell the major the two guides were actually enemies and didn't trust each other which they actually were.

Plan on meeting with the major in a few days. Let everyone settle down myself included. They all want to know what had taken me so much extra time to get back. Had to tell them two lower Chiefs were angry because, cause them to not to get all the goods they wanted. So had sent their best trackers out to kill me, to stop it from happening again. Also would bring much honor to the tribe to kill Brave Hawk a white man. My guide friend had warned me telling me the two chiefs were very angry with me. He said they had trackers but none could compare to Gonacheaw or you. Be careful, anyway they mean to have your scalp. He also told me he had packed up my belongings and had killed the other guide and used my clothing so that the Army would think it was me that he he had killed. This way the Army would not try to follow me. But the Indians would. They knew I wasn't killed. The two lesser chiefs were very angry if not for the main chief telling them all to leave, they would have accepted the so-called gifts.

Went to the Army compound looking for major Coel. The guard didn't know me, he sent another trooper to see if I would be received. The young lieutenant that went West came out and saw me he was very surprised. Told the guard I held a major rank to let me come in and he would escort me to the majors quarters. The major seeing me smiled and said it was hard for me to believe you were killed and very glad to see you have survived. He then offered me a drink of whiskey which it I turned down he told the lieutenant to sit down and me also. Then his next comment was what in hell happened. Proceeded to tell them what had come about. The major was angry that I had told the Indians he spoke with a forked tongue. Two of the sub chiefs were angry because the main chief turned down the supposed gifts and made the Indians leave. Decided this was not a very good situation for me and seeing made both sides angry. When I left found some of my clothes missing. The two guides were actually enemies. Had stayed with one guide and became friends. He also said the other guide would kill me if he had the opportunity. He also said he had caught him going threw my belongings and knew he had stolen some of my goods. He then said I will have to kill him before long. This situation I was very reluctant to get involved with, so packed up and left that very evening. What happened after I left had found out when returned to the city and family.

They were stunned to see me. The major then said leave it to the Army to screw things up and then laughed. I also said would have been back sooner but the two sub chief sent some of their best trackers to follow and kill me. Had to be extra careful on my way back. The major asked they were that upset with you. That wasn't the only reason I told him. He asked what was the other reason. Close my eyes for a second and sighed. You see the Indians know me as Brave Hawk if they could kill me it would bring honor to their tribe. I was an Arapaho and was not a part of their tribe, also I was a white man adopted Indian. Major also stated the word was that you were a hell of a knife fighter one of the troopers knew you and related a lot of stories about you. My answer major, the civilians are not above a lot of exaggeration. He again laughed and said some had to be true to be able to exaggerate. Just nodded my head in agreement. Then told him that he had sent some darn good men out west with me. They were excellent companions and good army men. Major said he was happy with his choice. He then asked why I had released his men before we got to the post. Had met a captain he told me that the major may insist that my escort stay at the post. This was not your orders but he would have insisted on his superseding yours. So rather than take a chance of that happening I release before we got to the post. The major nodded saying you made the right decision. I knew the major you're talking about he was not a good man and more than likely got what he deserved. I then took the papers out he had given me to turn over to him. He then said want you to keep them, they are official papers and properly stamped. You may never use them again but maybe you will. He then said would love to have you with me and would trust you with my life. This is one of the nicest compliments had ever received. Then he said sometime would like to hear the whole story. Then he must have thought I had killed the other major. Decided when and if we were to get together again would tell him the truth. The lieutenant sat there with a big smile on his face nodding his head. What a relief for me to have a man as sensible as this major.

Decided to ask Jan and Henry what they thought of asking the major and his aide the lieutenant to an evening meal. They would be thrilled but would still ask. Henry and Jan were thrilled, also wanted to know what my opinion was of them were. My answer was, they were both honest men. Not like others that looked to get promotions by any means.

Made it a point to stop at the post, when I approach they came to an attention and saluted me. As a common courtesy saluted them also. The major and the Lieut. were both on post. The major in his office, the Sgt. escorted me to his office and knocked on his door. Then told him who was here to see him, was directed to enter. The major stood and held out his hand in friendship he then asked if he could pour a drink. Turn him down. He then asked if I was against a drink, answered no would have a glass of wine sometimes or two but that was my limit. Informed him didn't care for the feeling that accompanied a lot of whiskey. Found would give some men extra boldness, some much to their detriment. He laughed and said have a few in the stockade because of their excesses with whiskey. His comment was new you were quite sensible. Told him wasn't very religious person but couldn't stand a lie or a braggart. He laughed and then said if anyone has a right to brag it would be you. The Lieut. walked in at that moment, he was now wearing captain bars. Had to congratulate him. He then thank me for the things that I had taught him on our trip out West. He also said he had had the opportunity to ask what I had thought of the major that was killed. My answer was he was a terrible man, none his men respected him. He was always berating his officers and insisted ever one was to salute. Told him this wasn't advised out here. His answer was they will salute. If it came to a battle the Indians would know who to go after first. He wasn't about to listen to any advice. He was also trying to trick the Indians to sign papers for land in exchange for the goods he had. This is when I informed one of the higher Chief's, he then had his brave throw goods to the ground. Made the other two Chief's also leave. This is when I decided to leave I had upset the major and also the two lesser chiefs. Would have to watch my back the on the way home. guide warned me. They would send their best trackers to take my scalp. This is why it took a lot more time for me to get back. The major said the Indians tried to kill you. Two lesser chief's were very upset with me for them losing all the so-called goods. The guide that was a good friend also told me that the other guide, he would have to kill because he is betraying the Indians for his benefit. Now was time for me to leave, packed up and found some of my clothing was missing. That was all that was missing which surprised me. Had a good rapport with the enlisted men they were watching where I was staying. They said if anyone was to try to leave with any of my goods they would stop them. The guide who became a good friend said the other guide wouldn't dare to take anything. He wasn't very brave just a lot of bluster. The major and a new captain both said we would love to hear what actually happened on your way back. Just shrug my shoulders. The captain then told him major, no one is going to be able to sneak up on major bird. The major looked at the captain, the captain then said he knew in advance when we would meet a column of soldiers hours before. They showed up and he also knew when a lot of individual coming hours ahead. He had us hide until it was safe to move again. The captain then said we heard a shots and you never really told us all that had happened. Will sometime I will relate more. Told them was inviting them to dinner, would also invite the two enlisted men who went out West with us. One his service time was up and he laughed. The other ones time was almost up and was on leave. Before I left decided to tell the Major and

Captain the truth of what had happened. Will now tell you what really happened to the major out west. I had pact up ready to leave. The Major sent his orderly he would like to see me. I knew he was up set, would be careful of what I said not to upset him any more. Went in to his office, my guide I had be friended was standing next to him the Major being seated at his desk. His next comment was my other guide told me I was speaking wit a forked tongue. My answer was you were. He then raised his hand with a pistol and said I'm going to kill you for that. My Indian guide new what he had planned and put his had on the pistol forcing it down and cut his throat at the same time. He took the pistol and told me I was to go out with my hands in the air. He told me the other guide was dead and in my clothing He said want the army to think it was you they would think it was you that had cut the majors throat because of your knife being so obvious. Had already pact. He had brought my ponies to where the other guide was laying and mutilated to look like it was me there. Then we both left on a trail he knew well. Rode day and night for 5 days. Was going to go with him to meet my brother Gonacheaw. He told me not to. Gonacheaw said would do more good in the white mans places. Then told me the chiefs were very angry would send their best trackers for your scalp. This is why it took me so long to get back.

And this is when I said will let you get back to your duties. Be back to let you know when the dinner will be.

Henry had said we will invite some of our friends also we may as well have a get together with all. Our banker friends heard you had been killed but now are back. Everyone wants to know what had happened. Mom Sue Jan did all the organizing, Henry took care of all the invite. Laura Lee and Bell were busy with their agendas. Both were having a good time. Chad wasn't very happy Bell treated him like a brother as did Laura Lee. He finally realized that was the way it would be and came to respected this. Henry made sure it wasn't going to interfere with Bell and Laura Lee's performance. They were both selected to be in a production at one of the theaters both of our girls were very pretty. Jan had watched them rehearse and also gave them very good pointers. The director told Jan they would become excellent actresses because they were willing to learn and had a lot of confidence and really loved the theater.

Before our dinner we had planned ,the girls were to perform. We all made sure we were there and had the best seats. This was a comedy, girls didn't have major parts but did very well with the parts they had. The crowd gave all a standing ovation. We all were thrilled how well it had gone over. There were other programs scheduled, would be a few weeks before they had another performance. We went backstage and were introduced to the playwright and director. Jan and Henry also decided to invite them to our dinner party. They accepted. Couldn't get over how well the two girls acted out their parts. Jan Henry myself the rest of the family would do all we could to encourage them. One part of the play had one of the girls play a snooty part. She was to put her nose in the air and turn away in a huff. One of the other actresses stepped on her gown which tore away leaving her in her petticoat. This was quite risque and the audience roared as she squealed and departed the stage on the run. Guy Bess and Chad were there, Chad had brought a girlfriend with him. Chad was like a son to Jan and myself we were glad he had realized Bell was not interested in him only as a brother. Chad introduced us then told his girl his two sisters were in the play. He looked at us and smiled we just grinned and nodded. He told his girlfriend we were his second mom and dad. We invited our group out to a late evening meal. Knew where I had always stayed before, and they had served meals in later evening hours. The evening went well.

Decided to hire a bodyguard for the two girls. We couldn't always be at their side when they were rehearsing. The manager at the theater suggested a man, he was quite large and intimidating. Made arrangements to the theater to pay him. Less then a couple of weeks or two girls came into the house all excited and upset. What was wrong,

132

then they proceeded to tell us what had happened. The rehearsal went real well. Just a short ways out of the theater as Bell and I walk by one of the alleys on our way to catch a hack. Two men stepped out and one grab Bell by both arms. The other grab me but only got a hold of my left arm. I knew what you and showed myself and Bell about such as an attack. My knife was out in a flash and I stabbed him in his lower chest. He let go of my arm then spun and stabbed the other one in the lower back. He let go of Bell and she stabbed me in the lower chest also. We then see our bodyguard stop we believe he had set this up. When they told me this. I normally carried my knife on my left hip and headed for the theater. When I got there the bodyguard was still there talking to some of the theater help. Walked up to him and said the next time I see you you're a dead man. Already had my jacket wrapped around my arm. Turned and walked away. He had pulled his knife and charge at my back. This is what I had expected of him. Then just spun to my right my jacketed arm pushing his arm aside my knife went into his neck wouldn't meet him again. Blood from cutting his artery was spurting all over. The theater help were bug eyed at what had just happened. This is when I wanted to know who hired him as a bodyguard for my two daughters. They were still bug eyed but could tell I was still upset. Finally one of them blurted out he isn't here right now will be here tomorrow morning. You people can call the police and take care of this mess you will find a couple of more men not too far they also will be dead. Still angry and upset highered man as a bodyguard and he sets up to attack and more than likely to kill both girls. Tomorrow would find out who had hired him. Next morning the police chief we knew quite well was there early. We invited him to breakfast he readily accepted. Bird he said you had one hell of an evening. We found two men not too far outside dead and another in the theater. The theater people who told me how he had attacked you from behind and in a flash this guy's throat was cut. They were still cleaning up when I left. Then proceeded to let him know had hired this man as a bodyguard and he had set the two girls up to be raped and he was planning to get in on the action. The girls said he just stood back and watched. The girls had been taught by me how to handle them selves in such a situation. If I hadn't taught them they may not be alive now. The chief then said Bird when they mess with your family it doesn't turn out well for them.

Then he said all three of these men were known criminals. We never had enough proof to catch them. This time know one has too worry about these three men. The chief then said, the man that hired a bodyguard showed up while I was there. He really thought this would be a good bodyguard he did chores around the theater and was very strong. Next time will have to check him out my self. Will find who is trustworthy and darn good. During breakfast the man from the theater showed up, could tell he was upset and scared. We invited him in also offered breakfast. He was all apologies. told him then it was more my fault for not checking this man out. Could see him relax. He also wanted to know how the girls were. They had not got up as yet. Bell had one arm that was bruised but both came out of the ordeal fine. The theater told me you killed all three. The girls took care of the two attackers themselves while the other was just plain stupid. Let them know at the theater the girls can take care of themselves. They have been trained. He then said the girls killed the other two. Just said they have been trained to protect themselves and yes they did. Well I will spread the word around and others will think twice before trying anything and also who their father is. Realizing the theater officer had thought he was doing a good thing. He then said learned another lesson. My comment was also had learned.

The girls came downstairs ready for breakfast, everyone wanted to know what had happened. They related their story not knowing the bodyguard was also no more problem. They also commented that bodyguard dad will have to get rid of him. The chief said your dad took care of that last night with a big grin. The theater officer said your dad did him in last night he tried to stab Bird in the back and got his throat cut. The two girls jaw dropped, then said we knew dad would take care of that situation. They then asked if they had caught up to the other two who had attacked them. The chief said you girls took care of them. They look kind of questioning, the chief said they are both dead the girl said we believe they really meant to hurt us so we fight back the way dad had taught us. The kitchen help Henry and Kate kept shaking their heads. Henry spoke up saying thank God they are okay and you to Bird Jan just gave me a squeeze on the arm. She was busy with the girls when I left, she didn't really know what had happened with me until the police chief showed up.

Jan said Bird why didn't you tell me what had happened to you last night. Jan you were taking care of the girls didn't want to upset you anymore. She then said because of you we always come out all right, and proceeded to give me a hug.

The dinner were the major and now Capt. was about ready to happen. Jan and I had hoped not too much of the word about the girls would get out. Was anxious to get back to the farm, thanks that we had such good help. A lot of the companies we had started were still giving us a good profit. The pipe we were making we had a hard time at the mill to keep up. Would have to install extra machines to take over the extra load. This part of our business was the part I love so well, the smell of the wood of the mill was like perfume to me.

The blacksmith shop was still giving us a profit were setting the funds aside for our blacksmith friends. Knew they were going to stop working before long. Where had the time gone. Chuck decided to turn the Smithy over to them so they could sell two younger crew if they had a mind to. We also told them our bank was holding money in their names. They question what money, they had not started a bank account. Chuck Chum and myself just laughed and Chuck said well someone did. There is a substantial amount in your account. They both asked if there was enough to build a new house just outside of town. They had bought a small plot of land and would like to build on it. We all agreed that that is Chuck Chum and myself would put them up a house. They gave us their plan saying they hope they would have enough money. We then showed them what we had put aside for them at the bank. There were astounded, the share we had collected all went into their account. We looked at their plans and found very modest. Then told them there wouldn't be any problem putting their house up. The three us grinned we would put up a lot fancier home than they had expected. What good men they were and darn good friends. As we last mentioned have not had much preacher problems. They broke out laughing say we should have hung the blackard anyway. Chuck said we always seem to get more work but this is one we will really enjoy.

The dinner for the major and a Capt. was all set up, we had all our friends coming. The bankers wives and other business people. Would be quite a gathering. Henry and Kay decided to make a big dinner instead of a luncheon. When all arrived some early, Henry had set up a cocktail he knew a few would drink too much and could spoil the dinner, so it was a mild but very flavorful. Seems like we always have someone show up that wasn't invited. He had asked where the drinks were. Henry told him that cocktail was the only drink he had his next move was over to the bowl and start dipping his cup in and gulping one cup after another this upset me, Jan held onto my arm saying Henry will take care of this. Henry had went around to our guests asked if and when had invited him. The two bankers the and said no he comes to get free drinks when he hears it at of the dinner. Henry then had the man from the barn come and escort him out and not to gently, he tried to mouth off but a poke in the gut shut him up and out he went with very little commotion. The dinner went real well after this episode. The men now ready for their drinking and cigar. Was thankful was a warm summer evening. The

Windows being opened would dissipate most of the smoke. The major asked me to fill him in what had happened on my West trip. Some of the men had not heard that had made a trip back out West. There were only six or seven of Henry's close friends that had stayed for drink and cigar including the Major and the Captain. Some had the word that I had been killed and wanted to know what had happened.

Well this major was trying to get the Indian Chiefs to sign away their land by giving them blankets a lot of trinkets and whiskey. When they had gotten together there were two sub Chiefs and one that would control the gathering. Told them the major was not giving them gifts when they put their Mark on the paper they were be giving him their land. Both the guides were there also. The one guide and I had become good friends with. He knew who I was and said my brother was on under the grisly when you killed it with your knife. Told him things get exaggerated, he said no was there when it happened. The woman had filed into the room and Jan hearing my comments said I was there also know why the Indians call him Brave Hawk. Oh that's kinda getting away from what happened. My guide friend said pack up and leave. The major will be very upset. The other guide will tell him with sign what you told the Indians. The main chief had thrown all the goods to ground. Then making all the Indians leave. Could tell also the two under chiefs were really upset with me, also my guide friend said will kill the other guide. He will be telling the major what you had told them he spoke with a forked tongue. Packed up and headed out what was surprising was some of my clothes were missing. Two days out my Indian friend caught up to me. He then told me had killed the other Indian guide dress him in my clothes so the Army would think it was me. He also killed the major when he had attempted to shoot me. Then he said the Army will not bother you they will think your dead but the two Indian Chiefs will send out their best to kill you and take your scalp and belongings. Then mentioned would travel with him to see

Gonacheaw. He then said no he had talked with Gonacheaw and he said you should not. The younger bucks don't know you and they are now riled up. You may do more good in the white man's world. We parted and I headed East for home.

Major then said that was not the end of it. What happened on your way home. Your guide friend warned you about the other two Chiefs. Well was his next comment. Kind of sighed and said they had sent out men to kill me. Had not told anyone this part of this trek. Will tell a short version what happened. Five Indians were following me made a lot of detours trying to discourage them. They still kept up. Left my ponies and decided to confront them. When I stepped out in front of them on the trail the older one dove into the brush the other two tried to shoot me killed them both then left hoping they would quit. Decided to find a camp and see what they were up to. The tracker was telling them his pony had dumped him or he would have killed me. this is when I stepped out saying I was here now. He went for his rifle of my arrow went through his heart. The other two just started their death chant. Calm them down tell them if the quit following me I would spare them.

They then told me to others were also following me from the other tribe. He was an older tracker and very experienced. Now would have to be double careful. The next few days they tried to set up an ambush. Could always sense where they were in what leisurely change my route making them think they were having bad luck. Then made up a day camp as though I had thought was now safe. Took both my rifle and bow. Made out as was going to hunt for rabbit or grouse then made a fast loop onto an opposing Knoll to watch. To my surprise they came in after an hour or more, the older man set up in some brush not too far from my set up the younger on the downside of my camp. My fire had not been lit making them think when I got back with my kill would start the fire. Made my way back around and waited till dark. Then crawled for over an hour. Stopped in a slight dip in the land and proceeded to knock an arrow. Looked and he was sitting very still he then turned just as I let the arrow fly and hit him in the chest. Heard him groan knew he still had his rifle So made quick rollback in case he had a sense where the arrow had come from. He just hollered out Brave Hawk you killed me don't kill my son. He then called his son to him telling to put aside his rifle. His son came to him and laid his rifle the ground. The older tracker had his son move both rifles and lean them against a tree. Then stepped up to then check on the older man. Asked if he was spitting blood and said no.

Then told his son the fire makings were beside the pile and get it started then told the older Indian he would survive would remove the arrow cut the arrow to make sure there would be no splinters when it was pulled out. My arrows were made on a small lathe were very smooth. Cut the arrow with my knife and then pulled it back out we had hot water going and washed his wounds he still was not spitting any blood. His son said father told me was sure you knew we were following. He then said now know the way you set up this camp to ambush us you surely knew. We became blood brothers before they traveled. He told me he would kill the chief for me, told him not to just let him know we are brothers he will not be chief very long. You and your son will take over his spot. Felt bad knowing the Indians were in for a tough time. Nothing I Would be able to do about it.

The rest of the way just avoided all that came up to trail traveling down. Was surprised to find was considered dead the Indian my friend killed didn't look like me. The captain spoke up telling me the body was badly mutilated and dressed in my clothes. They assumed it to be me. The captain that took over the majors post wrote saying why he had killed me couldn't understand we seem to be good friends. In a separate note off the record he had said the whole detachment was glad to see the major gone. A couple of the men asked how in the world that I know the Indians were following me. Jan spoke up telling them was trained by one of the best trackers of all the Indians. He taught Bird, Brave Hawk as the Indians know him all these things they are brothers. Very few Indians have this power, Gonacheaw passed it on to Bird. One of the men could tell was very skeptical saying how and blank did you he just pass it to you. Then told him for over a year would be just the two of us he tell me what and how to read sign and then just think back to see if someone was tracking us, also to think ahead for an ambush. Trial and error learned quite well. He taught me, telling me because was born white would have a lot harder time to survive if I didn't know these things. He would always say was better than he. Knew it was his way of complementing me. Never would come up to his capabilities. One of the other men spoke up saying my son is a very good tracker, when he was six or eight he came across an old man they liked each other. The old guy took him under his wing and taught him a lot his knowledge. My son is in the woods when ever he can be. He now has to work with me at our company. I'm sorry he didn't come to this is dinner. He had said it would be just a bunch of old men smoking cigars. When I relate what had happened he will be sorry he missed this dinner. He then asked Bird will you and Jan come to our house for dinner so my son can meet you. Of course your daughters and the rest of your family also. Jan said we would love to. Another man said you were shot off your horse a while back why didn't you sense him. I just shrug my shoulders, Jan spoke up telling Bird did he turned to his left to watch this man. By turning the bullet from his gun hit Birds knife and up in his left arm. If he had not turned he would not be with us now. Also Bird told me after he knew something was wrong. That's why he had turned to see what he was up to. Just that look back saved Birds life. A lot of the other men just nodded.

Mom and Sue chum and Chuck were heading back to the farm. Mom and Sue they need to care for their herb garden. We had good men in the city taking care of our enterprises. They were paid well and were a good honest men Jan knew I was anxious to head back. She said Bird we will head back after we have dinner with the family that invited us. Jan said now we will have to talk Laura Lee and Bell into coming with us. Jan reminiscing said Bird don't know why we never had any more children. We both would have loved a boy. Well we have Chad and two beautiful daughters. Can't ask for much more. Well Jan said it would not be for lack of trying and laughed at her own comment.

Chum came to me and told me one of our men that was selling some of our goods, had some men forced him to leave were he was set up to sell. He checked after and found some one had moved into his location and was selling a lot higher prices. Chum said we own the store and property we had just better find out what is going on.

Chuck said he would take care of things at the farm in the sawmill. Mom and Sue said we need to check on our herb garden. Two weeks is too long to leave it unattended. Knew the help would do it for mom and Sue, they were just anxious to be back at the farm Jan and myself.

Told chum hard to believe some that bold would not expect repercussions. After the dinner the major who insisted we call him Cole invited us to a dinner. He also said Bird know what is on the Army record but would like to know what actually happened. This isn't for any record just my own peace of mind. I told him the story was very close to what had happened. Told Jan what Chum had told me and we would take care of this the next day. Jan said you and Chum be careful anyone that bold can be very dangerous. Chum and Chuck had both acquired revolvers. Chum said he would be caring his tomorrow. Bird you had best replace your knife with a revolver. The revolver is taken the place of a knife for self-defense. Had been thinking of doing so for a while. Next morning Chum and I went out to check on the store property. We couldn't believe that someone was trying to take over the store.

Our help went with us bringing a couple of his family who are not afraid of a fight. We walked in and let the man that was in charge know he had best leave as of now. Chum had his revolver in his hand, the man said will take my stuff. My answer you will take your men and yourself and leave. The merchandises is ours knew we had some of his own there he may learn a lesson from this. He realized he was outnumbered with some of hateful looks he and his two companions left.

Our storekeeper stayed in room in the back of the store. The two men who I came with him were his brothers. One of the brothers said believe know you and your knife fighting. Saw you when we thought you were afraid of this other knife fighter. He was well known doing quite a few in. Some were making bets but one guy knew you and was betting on you. He did real well with his betting. The fight lasted about a half a minute, he had challenged the wrong man and paid the price. This one man said was at the blacksmith shop when they needed extra help that's why I had seen the fight.

Our storekeeper said will pay my brothers to keep an eye out just in case he tries to come back Chum said we will pay them you won't have to take it out of your pay and commission. He spoke up saying he would pay half. Chum then said Bird you need a revolver now had to agree would shop for one. Chum then told me where to go. Found the place just on the outskirts of the city. The man who owned the place was an excellent gunsmith. Let him know Chuck and Chum had sent me. Told them I would like a small revolver that would be easier to carry a my left hip. This is where I carry my knife and not on my shoulder anymore. He smiled and then said you want what most call ladies gun. My question was if it's powerful enough okay if not will compensate. He then said no I have a revolver that has been made by me one of my favorites. He then went out got this revolver out. Couldn't get over the workmanship that had gone into it. Have fired this quite a few times it works well. Have a shooting range outside would you like to try it. He had a couple of men working for him they were also curious because most were apprehensive about shooting for the first time. He asked if I had ever shot a revolver no was my answer.

Just outback was his range for shooting revolvers and also rifles. They set up small blocks of wood on a board about 25 to 30 feet away. He had showed me how the revolver worked. He cocked the hammer back for each shot. Five shot revolver to reduce the size. Took my time raised shot cocked and shot again all five shots knocked the wood blocks off all five shot. One of the men said thought you never shot before. Turned to him and said never revolver. Bow and arrow and rifle. he then said if you shoot as well with a bow and rifle don't want to have you shooting at me. Jan came with us.

Jan had came with me and was in the shop looking over all the merchandise and equipment. Back in the shop one of the men said you sure are some shot with that revolver. Jan then said you should see him with his bow. He takes grouse on the fly with it.

Needed a holster that would fit well on my left side. One man asked why on your left your right handed. Just feels more comfortable for me and won't be so noticeable. Always carried my knife on my left. He then held the holster and revolver on his left. Then agreed would be be very good. He would make me a holster that would work on the left side. As we left asked Jan what she thought about buying a revolver for herself. Will have to come back to make up my mind. Most are too large for my taste.

We made arrangements to have dinner with major Coel at the post. He said the food was quite good. The new captain would be there also. Laura Lee and Bell were also invited but had their theater performance to attend to. We arrived were saluted and welcome to the post. The major and Capt. were waiting for us. We were offered drinks and accepted a glass of wine. The meal was served by the orderlies and went real well. After the meal the major said bird what did actually happened out West. Well after making both some of the Indians and the major angry with me decided would be best to leave. My friend the other guide said when the other guide told the major I had told the Indians he was speaking with a forked tongue. Two of the other Indian Chiefs were also very upset with me for spoiling them from getting all the goods. Had most of my belongings already pack. Found one set of my outerwear was missing, didn't give it much thought at the time. The major sent his orderly telling me the major would like to see me. When I walked into his office my guide friend was standing beside the major. Walked up to his desk. He said the guide told me you told the Indians I was speaking with a forked. Well you were was my answer. He then raised his hand from his lap holding a revolver, saying you will not be saying that again. My guide friend quickly put his hand on the majors forcing his revolver down and at the same time cutting the majors throat. Then he said knew he intended to shoot you me being the only witness. He then said your gear and ponies are loaded I will have you walk ahead of me so they will think that I'm going to kill you. When we got to my ponies the other guide was mutilated and dressed in my clothes. My guide friend said the Army won't bother you, they will believe it's you laying there.

The two Chiefs will send their best Braves, they don't know who they are trying for. We partied knowing would never see each other again. You know the rest of what happened was why it took me so much more time to get back home. The evening went well had to tell how I came to live with the Indians. The captain said you survived quite a few battles. Jan said mostly with white man, who thought Bird was an easy target. Most didn't survive.

When we got back to Henry's and Kay's, the girls were home and in the kitchen for a snack before bed. They had a good evening with much applause and curtain calls. Our next dinner would be at the gentleman and son he wanted us to meet.

A young boy came in out of breath asking for Chum. Chum was getting ready to go back to the farm. He came downstairs when Jan called to them. The young boy then blurted out had been trouble at our one location. He had been told by our storekeeper to let us know if he saw anything. He then told us the three men had come back to the store and there was some shooting. Chum looked at me and said we had better check this out. We both left Chum With his revolver in hand and me with my new revolver. We approach the store with a caution all seemed quiet. Chum hollered to hello to the store. Our storekeeper came out and said everything was okay. His brothers and he had been prepared for these men they knew they would be back. Two of them were dead, the other had ran off before they could get a bullet into him. He and his brothers were on unharmed. Our storekeeper had seen them coming and his brothers and he were prepared. When they came in with revolvers in hand we hollered a warning, they shot at me but was ready and ducked behind the counter my brother shot from the back with rifles killing two. The other took off on the run. This will let others with the same idea of taking over the store it isn't going to happen. We were both relieved that things had turned out okay. Jan was also relieved to see us back without any harm to us or our storekeeper. We had other stores would check and make sure they were okay.

Our dinner invite to Horace and his son was our next commitment. We had to talk Laura Lee and Bell into going with us. They didn't perform every night so planned out okay. We were met at the door by a maid who answered and escorted us to their sitting room. We were a little early, Horace came in all excited saying he had planned on meeting us at the door. His son would be here shortly. We were then offered a drink. We all accepted a glass of wine. Looking at our two daughters, was hard to believe they were now old enough to drink wine. Jan seem to know what I was thinking, smiled and nodded.

The house wasn't real large but looked to be quite comfortable within minutes we were all introduced to Lester who insisted we call him Less. Jan grinned at me to see Lester was surprised to see the two girls with us. He was a little tongue-tied when introduced to our two daughters Horace also had a big grin on his face. He had not met Laura Lee or Bell either.

We visited for a while then were called to the dining room. Horace and Les both sat the girls at the table holding their chairs. Horace then stated he had not seen our daughters before, he knew we we had two girls but thought they were much younger. Horse and Les both commented have we met before, you both looked familiar. Bell and Laura Lee asked if they had been to the theater. Both then agreed they had been to see different plays. Never expected to have two performers at our home.

The evening meal went well. The girls were asked about their acting. Jan and I didn't have much input. The girls were explaining how they got started and how well they were enjoying making others laugh or sometimes cry. When things got a little quiet Horace spoke up saying Less you have to talk to Bird about his experience with the Indians. Jan then spoke up saying yes they Indians call him Brave Hawk. Less said dad told me I missed all the happenings. The first question Less Asked, why do they call you Brave Hawk. Just shrugged my shoulders. The two girls said dad you have to tell. Looking at Jan grinned and nodded. Proceeded to tell them because of a brave thing I did. Jan grinned saying bird tell how it happened, the girls both said we aren't even sure how it happened dad. Answering all right. Told him was adopted in the Arapaho tribe was one of the smaller encampments. Was attracted to the chief's younger sister and were planning on marriage.

When the word got out to the other Indian villages, a large Indian and two other braves showed up, bringing their ponies and other gear. He was going to try to pay for my Indian maid to marry him. All the kids just stayed away from him. Could tell he wasn't liked. My adopted mother had packed up my belongings and wanted me to leave, telling me he was here to cause me trouble. Could see he was watching me all the time. Others had spread the word about me knocking two arrows out of the air that were meant to kill me.

Myself I really didn't know at the time he had planned to make a challenge for me to fight him. A few of days past a lot of tension. Next day he positioned himself close to the food as I walk by he poked his tomahawk out wanting me to bring him some food. Then turned and spit on him, all hell broke loose, him hollering and swinging his tomahawk. The woman of our camp came out got in front of me to stop him from coming with his tomahawk's. Little arrow was right by my side he was my now Indian brother. My Indian mother grabbed my arm and tugged on me to leave. So went back to tepee with her. She told me then I must leave this brave had already killed six or eight braves. Figure have to watch my back.

That afternoon the Chief called for me, went to him he then told me this Indian had come to him telling I had insulted him and he was challenging me to a fight. Just shrug my shoulders telling the Chief would face him. My Indian maid then said she would leave with me to avoid the challenge. The chief then said if you do leave you won't be able to ever stay with us you will have to find another tribe that will except you.

Had no intentions of leaving. Had been watching him also he just looked like a big braggart and look to me to be a little awkward at that. Told the chief wasn't leaving. They set up the challenge for the third day. My Indian maid insisted we would go out to her favorite spot a little pond. She was worried would get into trouble in the village. She was also trying to convince me to leave with her. Refused saying was not to be, coward. The two days passed rapidly my Indian maid just push me away when tried to get into her sleeping blanket. She just shook her head no. The next day Gonacheaw came for me. Then asked him what was expected of me. He then told me there would be of 30 to 40 foot circle drawn. When I was ready step into the circle. Then my challenger would then step into the circle and the fight to the death would begin.

Gonacheaw I could tell was upset we had become good friends he was teaching me to track. Others had heard about the challenge and there were a lot of strangers that came. Even the Indian who had shot arrows at me. Didn't know this at the time, he was saying to his friends he was sure that he wouldn't be able to kill me. Found out later they just laughed at him. My Indian mother was on the knoll overlooking the fighting circle. She stood with her arms folded and looking very proud. My Indian maid had disappeared the day before. When the time came Gonacheaw came for me. The circle was surrounded by Braves, if either tried to get out of the circle they were pushed back in. The chief handed me his tomahawk knowing I didn't have one. Just had my knife. When I got to the circle the big Indian was on the other side he had a smirk on his face, he thought I would be another easy kill. I then stepped into the circle. He waited then stepped in raising his tomahawk's in the air letting out a loud war whoop. I was already making my my move three large paces leaping into the air caught his tomahawk with my tomahawk twisting and driving my knife into his neck and down into his chest. His next move was to drop both his tomahawk and holding his hands out to the two Brave that he came with. They turned and left. The people on the knoll had not even settled in and the fight was over. The chief and the shaman both knew I would come out victorious. Just before the fight the shaman gave me a nod and a slight smile. When the chief gave me his tomahawk he also had given me a nod and a slight smile. Having the tomahawk and knife still in my hands went to the chief and handed them to him he then went over and wiped them both on the back of the dead brave. Then came back and handed them to be. The two Braves that came with him had turned their backs and left the circle.

A big feast was plan even had I lost. The shaman and chief both knew what the outcome was. My Indian mother also predicted the outcome, including the Brave that had shot arrows at me had told his friends I would win. Again they had just laughed at him. My Indian maid also knew came to her in her meditation. The shaman then renamed me Brave Hawk.

Was very brave to face a Brave that had killed many others in the same kind of fight. Had attacked like a hawk by going into the air to make my strike. That's how it came about me being called Brave Hawk. Less then asked how I knew what to do. Then told him my father-in-law had taught Chum and myself how to fight. Also if you can strike first this would usually end the fight. Less then asked if I had killed a lot of Indians Jan spoke up saying Bird has had a lot of fights because he always favored the Indians. So more white men than Indians. Less then said you were trained to track by an Indian tracker, said I was he was the best. Jan again said on our trip out West Bird always knew when others were following or if we were safe from an ambush.

Jan then related her rescue from a bunch of buffalo hunters that had abducted her. How I had rode right into the group and picking her up on my pony and out safely the other side. Bird went back to stole all the horses. We later gave some to the Indians.

The evening went by quite fast. On leaving the Horace took me aside and asked if Less could asked the girls out for dinner. The girls make up their own mind if they were willing it's fine with Jan and myself. Less wasn't a real large boy but like myself well toned and not overly muscled. The girls were pleasantly surprised. They knew had told them that Horace's son had missed out on a great dinner and after dinner conversations we had had. Less had told his father, old men smoking cigars, he would forgo that. He was surprised to find Jan and myself a lot younger than he had it pictured. We were now considered elderly because of having two grown daughters. Less gave us a nice complement, he said you both don't look over 20 or 25.

After the meal we all went to what Horace called his sitting or gaming room. He had quite a few books also a table for playing cards or games. Wood stove for heat if need be. Horace had told his son about some of the things I had talked about, especially my Indian brothers and my best friend Gonacheaw. Less began telling about his former friend who had past on. How he had showed him a lot of the ways of looking at things, and tracks and how to be quiet in the woods. He then asked me about Gonacheaw. My next comment was he was the best tracker of animals or men and had taught me some of his lore. He also taught me to use my concentration to look ahead and also look back on your own trail. Not with your eyes but with a knowing. Told Less can not explain how he did this and pass some on to me. Gonacheaw could track someone on bare stone. Showed me what to look for also to feel how long ago the tracks were made. Animals were easy, men were a lot harder especially if they didn't want to be tracked. This had no effect on Gonacheaw's ability. When he was first teaching me had my nose almost a few inches from the rock we were tracking on. Finally was able to make out the outline of the footprint. Was almost like a halo around the step. We would be gone during this for two weeks or more. Little arrow would be making the tracks he was an excellent tractor himself. Gonacheaw then began to teach me how to sense anyone or a group following or tracking us. Then told Less about another thing he had taught me. That was too hide our tracks. We had stopped for a while, he then asked if I could feel anyone following us. Concentrated and told him that three maybe four were on our trail. He then said you now know how to do this, you can also do the same thing looking ahead. Now we will hide our tracks from the young Braves that are following us. They intend to surprise us. We will surprise them. We then just concentrated on hiding our tracks and made a circle coming in behind them. They were looking for our tracks when we approach them from behind. Gonacheaw just saying our tracks are behind you. They were startled to hear us so close behind them, not knowing we were there. Our tracks just seem to disappear from their site. Never tried this when riding a pony. I didn't use the tracking as much as I use the sensing for someone following or someone ahead. Jan then spoke up telling about how I knew four men were following us with bad intentions. Bird set up an ambush, all four didn't survive. Bird also rescued me from a bunch of buffalo hunters who had captured me when on a running exercise away from our camp. Made the mistake of not taking my rifle. Less had to know how that came about. Jan proceeded to tell how I rode into their camp running over one of the men, picking me up and out the other side. Bird also went back and corralled all the horses and came back with them. Less still wanted to hear more. Just said getting late the girls have a full date ahead of them so we will have to leave. On our way out Hoarse had a big grin on his face and just nodded and whispered a thank you.

Heading back to Jan's father's, Jan the girls and I reminisced at how the time had gone so fast. The girls now in their 20s and doing well in their chosen careers.

Jan in her 40s myself also in my 40s. The country in turmoil, the South calling to separate from the union. We had not paid much attention until everyone was relating to it. Jan and I prayed things would be settled without too much turmoil.

The girls both liked Less and were pleased we talked them into going to dinner with us. Less had asked them to a dinner outing. Both girls had suitors but none they had brought home to a dinner. Most they had mentioned were in the theater. The girl's said most were just stuck on themselves. A lot of the older men would ask them to dinner they had refused all. Seems the younger men associated with the theater were stuck on themselves and others were just looking for a good time. After the incident of them being attacked and killing both attackers, the invites were not forthcoming. They were now treated with some awe and respect. Both girls like Less he not only was a gentleman but was well read and was pleasant to talk to. There dinner invite had went real well both girls were surprised and pleased. Told Jan looks like we now have a real suitor on hand. Jan laughed saying it's about time we need a grandchild. Mentioned to Jan wish the girls had gone out to dinner with the new captain he is a good man. Well maybe was Jan's answer. The girls had concentrated on their careers, boys were just an afterthought. Now that they were well established and had became very popular and at ease with their careers it would more than likely happened. Less was the first one they had shown an interest in. Another coincident the captain and less were cousins and were good friends. Less had told the Captain about the dinner he had with Bell and Laura Lee. He was stunned at first saying he knew me very well and I was one of the best men he knew. Less was also impressed. Joel told of his experience with me out West, saying he knew things that were happening we couldn't explain. Knowing we would meet a detachment of Army in a few hours and it happened just as he said plus other things. He would not let the men smoke only when he knew it safe to do so. The Indians could smell and know where we were if we weren't very careful. He told us were invading their territory some aren't very happy about this, best to be cautious. Joel then asked Lester set up a dinner so he could also meet the girls.

Jan said it looks like the girls are comfortable in their careers, now maybe we'll have some grandchildren. My comment, too good men are interested. A lot of others also, but after hearing about the two men to they killed they shy away. Sure glad taught them how to protect themselves. They would not be with us if I hadn't.

The dinner went well a lot of good conversation Jan and I did some reminiscing saying you were almost killed when first married, was pregnant at the time. When she mentioned this all want to know what had happened. Jan spoke up saying Bird has keep t it totally himself. His good friend is the only one that knows. I would not have known except for the bruises and the wound on his head when he got back to the farm.

Was quite a while ago. Jan then said you never did really tell me all that happened. I said I wasn't proud of getting caught off my guard. The girls spoke up with one word. Well, all looked at me expectantly. Shook my head in just sighed. When the president was gathering the Indians from the South to send them West. Went south to see what was actually happening. It didn't sound good for the Indians. Guy asked if he could make the trip with me. Was glad to have the company. We arrived at a hostel ask Guy he would on pack I would take a look around. Went to one of the Army post to asked what was happening. Our orders are to remove all the Indians and head them West to new lands. An officer came out he told me no one was to interfere or be jailed. This was his orders. Then just went wandering around to see how the Indians were being treated. Came across four men actually throwing a family out of their house. Walked over saying it wasn't necessary to be so rough they just laughed, I turned to leave, instead of of backing away and was hit aside the head with a rifle held by the big one seem to be their leader. They all then kicked hell out of me. An older lady not an Indian came out and told them to stop. They laughed but did stop. She then poured water on my face wiping it off. The four men had left with the Indians in tow. She told me the Indians were good people and had befriended her. Those men would kill me if she hadn't interfered. Finally got my legs under me and stood up. Then asked where she lived. Was a small building more or less a shack. She was alone no family left. Then told her would be back. She said if you do don't go near them again they will kill you next time.

Guy was at the hotel waiting for me quite worried. One look knew had got into some kind of scrap. Had a bath drawn wash and cleaned the wound on my head. Guy asked what had happened and told him. Will confront these men and they will be more than surprise. Went into the meal room to eat. A few men were around asked him about the four men. A couple said they are mean blanket y-blank men. One said looks

153

like you had a run-in with them. My brother also got beat up by them, he's looking to get even. Told him would like to talk to him. Guy had left to go up and freshen up to our room. Looking for a table to sit at, all were occupied. One woman was sitting alone. Went over and asked her if it would be all right if I sat at the table. She was surprised and said a man was supposed to meet her here. He's very jealous and maybe angry. Looking at her could tell she had put powder on her face where her eye and face were bruised. I sat down saying will move as soon as there is another opening. Wasn't but a short while this man came in, could she the fear in her face. Seeing me sitting at the table with her he pulled a knife heading for the table cursing me hollering he was going to gut me. Stood up and pulled out my own knife twisting and shoving his knife hand passed my right side and driving my knife up into his upper gut and into his chest. A look of surprise on his face, he dropped his knife and I just push him through the door. He fell just outside the door. Walked back to the table telling the woman he would not be beating on her again she began to cry saying he had killed her young son when he had tried to stand up for her. Most had seen him come after me but didn't realize he was laying just outside the door on his face. Then asked if anyone would bury him would pay them to bury him face down. One man sitting at the next table said I thought you were a goner. How in hell you headed him for the door surprise hell out of me. Answered he was also surprised. The waiter was standing back dumbfounded. Sat down as he came over asked for whiskey and also if he knew of anyone who would bury him for me face down. He shook his head yes. Went over and talked to a couple of men they nodded yes to his question. Will pay them when they get back. The waiter brought a glass of whiskey, took it and proceeded to clean my knife then ordered supper for myself and the lady. She then asked if there was anything she can do for me. No but will do a little for you. Guy then came down and into the eating room. Sitting down said hello to the woman sitting with me. Notice everyone looking our way. When he looked at them they turned away. He then said Bird what the hell is going on. Shaking my head said I just killed a man. The two men outside the door were just now carting him off. Guy What happened. He tried to gut me with his knife. Guys comment was he made one mistake he won't make another again and I missed it. We then ordered supper for ourselves and the lady that was sitting at the table with us. We had finished our meal when the two men came back telling us that it was done and I didn't have to pay them. Insisted and gave them some coin. One asked then if the lady was now my woman. Just answered no she is now free of the madman. He then asked if she would be his woman saying he would treat her right. She agreed telling me he was a good man. We finished our meal gave the lady some coin to get her by for quite a while. Next day the waiters brother came to our room. He wasn't a small man, worked at of blacksmiths shop. Told him intended to approach these men again. This time will have my rifle with me. Will need backup, he was more than willing. He stated will scout and find the best place to confront them. Told him Guy and I would be packed up and head North after confronting them. Said don't think you have to worry, anyone would just think someone had it in for them. Then mentioned the old lady near the Indians home who had help me. The Smithy said he knew her. Want to do something for her and also you. Wasn't necessary was his comment.

Took a few days to get limbered up from all the bruises. Thankful nothing was broken, had some sore ribs not broken. Guy in the Smithy were watching the men. They were claiming the Indians belongings and selling them. Then would head for the saloon and drink. Guy said they are all caring rifles. We plan on approaching them at one of their hangouts. While Guy and the Smithy were scouting the four men out, went looking for an honest banker to set up funds for the Smithy and the old lady that had help me. Went to one of the banks and was directed to a lawyer. Went to see him, an older man and had asked around if he was honest. Then set up funds for the Smithy and the old woman.

Fifth day we decided to confront them. Their horses were tied outside went and took the horses and tied them where they couldn't be seen didn't have to wait too long before they came out. Guy was 10 to 15 feet to the side of me the Smithy on the other side, both like me next to a tree. With 30 to 40 feet away, they were looking around for their horses. Spoke up saying looking for something. Then told them all to drop their rifles. They all started raise their rifle my shot took the big man in the head, he didn't get a shot off next shot got the next one his rifle went off but went wild. Guy and Smithy took care of the other two. We then left going to their horses and unsaddled and unbridled them letting them free. The Smithy was going to keep them. Told him if the law gets in on this, they will know you were involved. I insist you need take coin from me and then told him to see this banker. Guy and I were on our way would not use the main track. Doubted if anyone would be following, made one dumb mistake and didn't need another. Back in the woods now and I was in my element felt bad to do nothing to help the Indians. Four evil men were not going to harm anymore anyway. Took our time and enjoyed our trip back without incident. Guy asked me if it disturbed me doing these men in. My answer was no they killed a lot of good people most wouldn't know how to handle this type of men. Actually felt better knowing they would do no more harm. Guy said Bird you don't seem to fear death. Again told Guy when my time comes will leave so far not before and just laughed.

Jan then spoke up saying bird because of your Indian friend you are always in some type of scrap.. The last few years you have calm down some. Laura Lee said dad you always come out on top. Bell and I are sure glad you are father. Jan said I am to, this got a big laugh out of everyone. The girls invited the boys to their next play. They readily accepted. Jan looked at me with a big smile raise my eyes and nodded. Henry and

Kay were also there. Henry spoke up saying Bird I wish I had been able to travel with you. My comment was, Henry you would have been one hell of a companion.

Jan and I were glad to see the girls finally showing interest in some young men. Jan then asked me if the young men knew the girls had protect themselves from a very serious attack. Knew that the word was out in the theater society. Maybe they don't know, Jan should we tell them. Jan then said they should be told. If it scares them off so be it. Will tell them the next time we meet. Jan I don't think they will be scared off. Still will tell them.

Henry and Kay were showing their age. Henry still got along well, Kay was having some problems she would just say she was okay. Henry looked at us and gave us a look that let us know Kay wasn't too well. The house and estate were still doing well. Henry had some real good people working for him. We always would talk to them. We were now wealthy but we never put on as though we were. The fruit trees were a pleasure to see. Some would produce two different types of apples the men were good at splicing one branch from one tree to another good producer.

Chuck and chum approached me to see if I would go to one of their offices to check out what was happening. Had received a message from one of our customers. The man in charge was holding up supplies unless they gave him a stipend. Next morning went early and looked things over a couple of the girls were already there. Just said good morning and went looking things over. Small room that was used for storage rearranged it for myself. Small room that wasn't being used set that up. Asked the girls were a good chair was. There was a couple in the main room that weren't being used. Brought that in and tried it for comfort. Wasn't great but would do. Then asked when the boss would show. He comes in around 10 or 11 o'clock. This upset me we were paying a good wage. Asked what their pay was they told me, it was half of what we normally paid. This manager was even knocking down on their pay.

Told the girls would be back later and not to mention me. Left found Chum telling him what was going on. He was stealing part of the girls wages The customers we had weren't happy some were looking else where for their supplies. Told Chum would go into the back room I had set up. Would insist on him come to the back room. Had Chum watch for him and come in shortly after. Went back and talk some more with the two girls. Found another girl came in with the manager. She was always turning them in for mistake she made. She was his mistress. Was not long when he showed up.

Before that Chum and myself at the bank had froze all the assets. They would check with the other banks for us and also have any assets frozen. Had the two girls tell him to see me in the back. He stormed in thinking I was one of the contractors. I had told the two girls to go in his office and use the chair to bar the door and wait for me or Chum to open up. He wanted to know who was making the demand to see him. He told me to get the hell out. This is when Chum showed up walking in and saying hello to me, saying to this man I see you have met my new boss. His attitude changed to a stuttering. I'm here to see you leave with your girl. His remark was will get my things and leave. Chum said no you will just leave. We will go through the office and what is yours we will give you. He turned and raced for his office, Chum just be hind him. When he found the door block, turned with a small pistol. Chum was close enough to force his hand to the side and forced him to drop the pistol. We had not expected this. Chum spun him around and twisted his arm behind his back. Will send for the police he began to cry and plead to let him go. You were about to shoot Chum and me and you expect us to let you go. Knocked on the door and told the girls was okay. His mistress had not shown up with him. Chum was going to send one of the girls for the police. Chum they know you I will stay. Had picked up his pistol. Told him to sit and was watching him closely. He spun around a small dagger in his hand. Surprise heck out of him with my knife at his throat. Told him don't want your blood on the floor drop the knife or will cut your throat. One of the girls with her eyes wide said I know you. Was there quite a while ago when you killed a man with your knife. He came at you with his knife in a flash he was down. My comment that was a long time ago. The police and Chum showed up, they took him off to jail. Chum had already filed a complaint against him. The girls also added he had pulled a knife on me was forced to drop it handed the knife and pistol to one of the officers saying the pistol is still loaded, he didn't have a chance to use either. Told Chum to take care what he needs to do, would stay and talk to any of the contractors that showed up. The girls had calm down some were still a little apprehensive told them to relax their jobs were not in jeopardy a contractor showed up, the girls were up and talked to him took care of his needs. He looked over and spotted me. Hello Bird glad to see you here I know you must have fired the blanket y-blank that was running this place for you. One of the girl said he pulled a gun on our big boss and he's now in jail. After the girls told our contractor what had happened.

We went into his office to look over the books as we said suspected two sets. He was stealing almost half the girls wages and also charging the contractors more and the extra was going into his account found he had two accounts. The third is our account where he was putting a lesser amount in our coffers. He just got a little too greedy. Chum said we will pay back our contractors and you girls will get your full pay. The third girl had not shown up. Told the girl to tell her she was done. One of the girls asked if she could throw her out. Chum and I totally agreed. Both girls went to work on the books, to organize and correct all the shenanigans the manager had caused. Chum said looks like the girls have been doing most of the work. Made my comment was, make one of them the manager. She took care of the last contract that was here Chum told her she was now manager. Both girls were astounded told her if she needed another girl she could do the hiring. Chum said he had hired this man on an others recommendation will chew him out.

Back at Henry and Kate, Jan was waiting supper for Chum and myself. Chum proceeded to tell what had happened. Everything had turned out all right. Henry said so many dishonest people thank goodness for the honest ones. Jan and Sue then said you two need to go to the farm for a while and relax. Jan said will be good for us to go to the lake and enjoy the woods and do a little fishing. We'll get things ready, Sue said Chum were all for going. The roads had improved so traveled by carriage, also much more comfortable. Mom seem to know we were coming and was waiting to greet us. Was good to see how well the farm was doing. Mom wanted to know how Kate was doing, Jan and Sue both said she is not complaining, but doesn't look well. Chum then said I'm going to soak in the tub after I get the water heated. Sue said will beat you there. We all had a good laugh, Jan then said Bird and I are next. This is one of our best loving sessions we had in a long time. So good to be home and able to relax. How fortunate to have a loving wife and family. Mom and Chuck were showing their age. Both were in excellent health Henry and Kate were having health problems. Henry had hired a manager for his farm and orchards quite some time ago. He was an excellent caretaker and treated the men and families like kin. So they worked well and did very good work. We were all worried about Kate she had her problems but could tell she wasn't feeling well. Mom Sue Jan Chuck Chum and I, at Chuck's asking for confab after our supper. Chuck then said and proceeded to tell us he had manager for some of our businesses. Our piping he had sold out under contract and that was doing well. Our sawmill had expanded and also had more business than it could handle at times. He said he and Chum had found a couple of good men to manage our affairs and keep track of things. They would file a report for himself Chum and myself. He and mom were going to do a little traveling back east and did not want to worry about our fortunes. Mom had a silly smirk on her face and just nodded. We were all surprised Jan and Sue had to give mom a big hug. Mom said Bird you now won't be the only one that travels.

Jan Sue Chum and I stayed at our lake cottage for a week. Wandered the woods enjoying ourselves. Made love often, we had not been this relax in a long time, seem so good. Chum and Sue decide to stay at the farm. Jan was worried about Henry and Kate, so we headed back to the city when we travel we rode our horses with a pack for our camping gear. We never stayed in any of the way inns. Most were infested with bugs and the food was just slop. We always stopped and moved away from the road so anyone could not see our camp.

Arriving at Henry's, found him upset. Kate was in bed and had not got up for almost a week. We went in to see her, she was propped up with pillows. Two of the maids were keeping her as comfortable as they could Kate welcomed us, then stated it was her time to leave. I've had a very good life and feel bad for my love Henry. Henry's comment was will follow you before long. Less than a week Kate crossed over. Henry had made arrangements everything went well a lot of crying by the help. She had treated all as her own family. Our friends the bankers and managers had set things up and made it a lot easier for Henry and Jan. A couple of weeks and things started to come back to normal.

Our two girls were doing really well and were very popular. They were thinking about the proposal the two boys had made. Would be great to have grand kids. Jan and I were hoping sometime soon.

We had always checked on our stores that we had in the city. Chuck and Chum had set up men that were now doing this for us. Gave Jan and I a lot of free time. We we would still run a few miles every day. We both enjoyed this. Henry would spend time in the orchard when the weather permitted, he would comment on the bees. How they work to make the honey that we enjoyed so much. We would sit with him quite often. At times would sit and reminisce about my Indian brothers. Jan would comment your thinking about the Indians, smile and nod yes.

We were always invited to dinner's, would accept most of the time. One dinner, the men talk about politics in our city. They mention I should just go and see how things were run. They knew a lot of corruption was going on. We know Bird you to be a fair man and honest. Mention this to Jan, she said will go with you. Would you was my question, of course was her answer. Not being involved in politics need some help in understanding the things that would have to know and understand. Was run something like a business. Hiring help for all the work to keep the streets up and all the other things related to keep things running smoothly. How the money is used and appropriated for the many things to keep running properly.

The one main politician was to introduce me as one overseer on the going on in the financial part of the city finances One big man was very belligerent he also carried a heavy cane. Was told not to cross him he would beat you with that cane. The last man quit after being beaten.

My next comment was will have to find a good stout cane, I know will be giving him a hard time. Had been told a lot of his goings on were questionable.

Later ask Jan if she would like to take a walk in the woods to look for a cane grown naturally. We spent a good part of the day and didn't find anything suitable. At dinner that night we were talking about the new job I had taken on. Jan then said Bird and I were looking for a natural cane for Bird to use in his new job. Henry then said have just what you want. Found this one quite a few years ago, it's really quite nice a little heavy but it can be slimmed-down. Henry went scrounging and finally came back with a cane. Jan then commented that you found that when I was a little girl should have remembered it.

It was a perfect cane for what may be needed for protection. Jan then told Henry why I would probably need the cane and not for walking.

Henry said Bird how you manage to get mixed up in some of these things is beyond me. My answer was always to try to do the right thing.

Was back in the city office and started to check on different things. Had Jan checking on the books and see where the money was going. All the paper work everyone was decent. Jan found a big discrepancy with this man's books. The books Were being kept by Another Man, went had a talk with him. He said I don't dare say anything to him. He beat the heck out of the last man that question him. When does he show up, he hasn't been here in a couple of days. He will be here tomorrow his money is running low. Who pays him, the paymaster and he's scared of him also. Well I will be at the paymasters and will confront him on the expenditures he has not turned in.

Nothing like a bill or any other expenditure. He claims he needs the money for such as street cleaning and other things he is supposed to be in charge of. When he comes in tomorrow will be at the paymaster to confront him. The man who tried to keep his books and the paymaster said you be careful, he's not going to like being confronted. My answer was will see what happens. Told the paymaster will confront him just outside your office. He has claimed pay for quite a few men. When I checked there were a lot less men on the payroll. This is what I will confront him with. Was hard to believe had so many crooks and not too smart either. All knew I was there just to find where the money was being spent and what for and why. This was the only manager we found to be gouging money. Also had informed the police what was going on. Was waiting for him when he came in the next morning. Was at the paymasters door blocking his entrance. Proceeded to tell him he was not going to enter or receive any more monies. He then said I will enter and raise his cane to cane me. Being ready for his actions warded off his blow and rapped him aside the head across the ear then rapped his knuckles he drop his cane. Then gave him a sharp poke to his side just under his rib cage knocking the wind out of him.

Jan had been watching with a few others. First time anyone had stood up to him that had not been beaten. For me it was an easy victory he was just a big powerful man, knew how to handle him quite easily. He left still grunting. Jan then came over saying Bird you were half his size and just took the wind out of him so fast some didn't see it happening. Jan said was a little worried when I see the how large he was. The new's spread fast.

Our two main banker friends came to the house that evening. They were all grins saying we had heard about your skirmish this morning that you took a few blows but managed to win. Jan then said Bird didn't to get hit even once, a couple of whacks and a heck of a poke in the gut and he was done. They were bound Henry Jan and I were to go to dinner that evening with them. The bets had been on the big man who had cowed everyone who had stood up to him. We made a tidy sum taking on bets on you so you see we owe you a dinner. Then they said bring your cane with you just for show. Jan started to laugh you really know Bird. They commented we knew he would handle this man with ease. My comment was will have to stop getting into these hassles.

The girls weddings was on our next agenda. Henry was beside himself getting things ready, we all could hardly wait for the event. The girls were all excited, but acted real calm, good actresses. The girls decided to wait for a couple of months and let everything settle down. They told me and Jan they wanted to tell them about the two men they had killed defending themselves, to find if this would bother the boys. They had waited for a couple of weeks, then at one of their dinners when the meal was finished. Laura Lee spoke up saying Bell and I have something to tell you about ourselves. The boys then just looked kind of curious. Both girls started to speak at once. They just laughed and Bell said Laura Lee will relate what happened. The boys just nodded. Laura Lee then told them they were attack and grabbed from behind. Laura Lee said he grab me by both arms from behind, he let go of my one arm to spin me around. Then pulled my knife and stabbed him in the lower chest, he then let go of my other arm could see Bell also struggling with the other man. I came behind and stabbed him in the back, Bell had also got her arm free and had also stabbed him in the gut. Our bodyguard had just stood back and had watch. Well that's what happened we decided we should tell you this. Both boys said yes we heard about this. They looked at each other and laughing, said we knew were asking two beautiful girls that could take care of themselves. So this is not any problem with us. Both girls relaxed then saying we were worried. Now we are really relieved. They then asked what happened to the bodyguard. Bell spoke up dad took care of him. Joel said figured your dad would not let him get away with the set up he had made with these two men. When the girls got home they couldn't wait to tell us everything went well.

Henry and his new cook and house manager had the arrangements all set up. Jan I said think I will just go hide somewhere. Her answer, Bird I would scalp you if you did that. We both had a good laugh over this. Laura Lee approached Jan asking can you talk dad into wearing his Indian clothes for our wedding. Jan said that outfit has been packed away for some time, will look at it and see if it still in real good shape. We'll see if I can talk Bird into wearing it. Both Bell and Laura Lee said we hope dad will where it. Shortly Jan approached me asking me if I would be willing to wear my original wedding Indian clothes. My comment Jan they probably are not in very good shape anymore. Will asked mom to get them out to see if they were worth wearing. The girls wedding would be at Henry's the honeymoon would be at the farm mainly at our lake.

Henry and his helper going all out to get everything in shape and all the arrangements together. Jan and I headed back to the farm. Mom had my outfit out and spruced up. Was surprisingly still in good shape. Wasn't crazy about wearing it. A lot of memories good and bad. Jan had to laugh when I put that outfit on. A good fit except for the britches were a little too tight. Mom said she could take care of that so it wouldn't be noticeable. Told Jan was hoping it would not be in such good shape. Will were it only because the girls asked.

The wedding day was approaching fast. The girls plans were to be married at the same time. Would walk both down the aisle at the same time. Jan was real pleased with this, myself also. I had thought the wedding would be at Henry's. Both girls said dad Henry's is not big enough. We will have a lot of our fans and theater associates.

I knew the girls were very popular because of their acting. Mom had me try the britches on-again. Amazing how she had sewn in small patches and they look like the part of the outfit. Had to admit was still in remarkable shape. The wedding day all the coaches were lined up at Henry's. A lot of hustle and bustle going on but was going quite smoothly. The girls would be the last in line to enter the church. Jan would be down front waiting for me to escort the girls down the aisle. The ushers had everything under control. Walked down the aisle a daughter on each arm. The two boys now men were standing with very serious expressions. Was amazed the church was packed Henry had set up a buffet for those not invited to the house. My thoughts were how fortunate we were to be able to do these things. Deposited my girls to the altar with their waiting men. Jan had a smile that was great for me to see. Well we would welcome grandchildren. The ceremony went well with a lot of well wishes. The girls had asked their new husbands before hand if they would be willing to go to the buffet to greet a lot of fans and a lot of their associates of the theater. Jan and I accompanied them also. We also got a lot of congratulations.

Jan and I also overheard one gentleman tell some of the younger boys and men that I was a knife fighter before the revolvers came into play and had killed up to 40 or 50 in different knife fights without ever being stab myself. Thinking to myself my Indian outfit is giving the wrong impressions. Wanted to move away but was hemmed in. He also stated he was at some of the fights. He had lost money the first time he had bet on the other guy and loss. Did not lose after that. Jan just looked at me and grinned. Jan thought that would be all forgotten by now. The guy kept on talking saying one of the knife fighter's had a knife in each hand. This is when I thought I would lose my bet. He then went and picked up a dead branch in his left hand and waited. When the other guide came at him he made a quick jump using this stick to push the others knife aside and at the same time cut his throat.

Jan we've got to move heard a lot more than I need to hear. Jan just kept excusing ourselves to make a path. The girls were still acknowledging a lot of fans. One of our banker friends spotted us and welcomed us over to his table. He had helped set up some of the buffet. We moved behind the table with him a big relief for me. Was always uncomfortable in a crowd. Jan told her friend Birds Knife Fights over the Years Are Still Being Talked about. Our friend then told us a lot had asked about the outfit I was wearing. He then just told them I was an Indian and then said he added adopted and laughed. Jan I knew there would be a lot of questions.

The buffet went on for a couple of hours when the girls then decided to leave us. Our friend then said you can ride with me in my coach if you would like. We would but our ride would wonder where we were and probably would get quite upset. Our friend just nodded in agreement. The house was also filled with the invited guest the tables were set and the meal was ready to be served. The married couples were nowhere to be seen we knew they were packed and were probably on their way back to the farm and Lake.

Mom Chuck Sue and Chum had left after the ceremony. They wanted to get everything ready at the lake cabin. Well supplied with whatever they might need or maybe want. In case of rainy weather all kinds of card and table games. A lot of different books. Mom and

Sue were avid readers they had a good assortment of books the Bible included. Both went by the goodness of the Bible and left out all the bad things knowing it was written by men. Jan and I also enjoyed reading but seem to always have something on the go so I read a lot less than mom and Sue. Wasn't long before Henry informed Jan and I the couple were on their way to the farm. We had stayed behind to accommodate all our guests. The meal was started all were being served. Henry had seen to the setting up in the meal being served. Jan also talked with our new cook. She had also arranged for extra help to serve the meal it was quite elaborate. Turkey goose duck chicken all could make a choice or a little each. We had asked some of our friends to be greeters they would know who to let in and turn away. Too many scoundrels would try to enter. A lot just to cause some kind of commotion to upset everyone. The meal and evening went real well. Some of the talk was about the states in the South that were going to secede from the union. Henry who kept up on the affairs told Jan and I there is going to be a war over this, doesn't look good. We had ignored the stories and what Jan I thought were rumors.

Our friend the major who is now a Colonel also said he and Joel would be involved before long. He also stated Bird you would be a hell of a scout for us if if and when this comes to pass.

Jan looked at me just rolled her eyes saying Bird you won't be able to go and be of assistance. Being middle-aged Jan and I were still in excellent shape. Most would tell us we can't believe you to have two grown daughters. We both knew are running and our out door and away from the city air was our best benefit. Told Jan going back to the farm and take a pack and wandered the woods for a while. Her comment was I'm going with you we both need a break from all the city. Henry overheard us saying if only I was able to get around better would love to go with you. My comment was welcome along. Henry just laughed saying having a very hard time to just walk in my garden without a cane hell to get old.

His next words were how fortunate Jan is to have you Bird, my comment oh no Henry how fortunate I am to have Janet and you. Jan just gave me a poke on the arm. We all laughed.

Henry had served just wine a lot of the men like their whiskey. A few would always overindulge. Henry had hoped this would curtail some of this. The few just drank a lot more wine. They also had a couple men with their carriages to help them into the carriage and home. The evening finally came to an and our cook came to us asking if all was satisfactory. We all told her how well she had handled everything. Ask Henry where did you find this cook she is another treasure. The cook blushed and stammered a thank you. Henry then said tell all they will get bonuses for their hard work. All did a heck of a good job. Jan and I headed for bed taking a bath to get rid of the cigar smoke. Henry's help had anticipated our next move. The bathtub was filled with hot water we both climb in for a good soak and scrubbing we would also scrub down before getting into the tub for a more pleasurable soak. Our lovemaking again was relaxing and loving. Crawled into bed just held each other til sleep over took us.

Woke up to a beautiful morning, birds were really singing. We just laid a while made love again before getting up. Jan said bird I don't know why we never had another child, just shrug my shoulders. After breakfast packed up and headed for the farm. Was good being back to the farm. Everything was running very well, the crops were excellent this year. The help we had were also excellent had the know-how to see things ran smoothly. We didn't keep a large herd of cows, and only had 12 or 15 milker's. Milk was one of our staples. This was just for our farm. The crops were the source of a good income. Mom and Sue with their herb garden also was welcome in the city at a good profit... Our sawmill was still going full blast sold a lot of the lumber to the city. We had refrained from cutting timber on our own land. A lot of the logs we would buy. We would also saw and keep the share of the lumber for the sawing. Worked out well for the loggers they in turn sold lumber and would cut more logs turning a good profit.

Jan and I stayed at the farm for a few days getting caught up on the local news and farm gossip. We packed up for a week or more living in the woods. Went well, our tent was big enough for the two of us. We enjoyed watching wild life, no one had done any hunting for some time. Was able to watch without us disturbing too much. Used my bow to kill a Partridge for one of our meals. A rabbit for another one. Deer sign also bear sign.

We came back to our lake and cabin after four or five day trek. We both stripped and went into the far end of the lake knowing the married couples were at the cabin. Lake was not a warm Lake stayed in for quite a while and swam hard to keep warm. Came out laid in the sun to dry off. Jan stated Bird with all your scars you have, I wonder yet how you have survived. Looked at Jan and just grinned, she then pounced on me, both of us laughing. Making love in the woods wasn't our first time. Went back into the water and swam for a while. Came out and let the sun dry us off before getting dressed again. We decided to pay the cabin a visit see how our couples were doing. When we came out of the woods we surprise them. The bugs weren't too bad so they were outside also enjoying the sunny afternoon. Laura Lee said should have known it was you and mom. We heard the noise from the other end of the lake. Jan said we didn't think we were making that much noise. Bell said we had heard voices and wondered who was trespassing. We visited for a while and Jan said will head back to the farm. They all spoke up, stay for supper we have cooked up a good meal. Joel and Less have found a honey tree and it looks like it's full of honey. Our hives did produce quite well but extra honey would be welcomed. Some of our farmhands were good at getting the honey without too many stings. The meal was very good Jan and I had not eaten overly much on our woods trek., So welcomed the meal. They all asked if were going to stay the night, we both chimed in saying no. Jan said Bird has not been to the sawmill for some time. Plan on going tomorrow.

The farm was about a mile or so from our cabin. We packed up and left wishing them well. Joel and Less stating we would have loved to hear some of your stories. Laura Lee and Bell both saying dad you have kept a lot to yourself. Jan said some I don't even know about. Joel then said heard you killed the grisly with your knife. Jan said he did I was there. Just rolled my eyes and shrugged. Jan laughed and said Bird won't say anything unless we really push him into it, but I know why the Indians call him Brave Hawk.

We got back to the farm and headed for the bathtub. A hot bath was always welcome. Chuck and Chum had went into the town, someone had come to the farm with some news that didn't sound good. Mom and Sue had not heard what it was about. After our bath, Sue had made us a cup of her and mom's herbal tea with honey. Wasn't long before Chuck and Chum came back. News was it sounded like a war had started between the North and South states. Chuck said we will most likely be hearing from the Colonel for Joel to be heading back to camp. Mom and Sue chimed in hoping it wasn't serious.

Jan was upset this doesn't sound very good to me. I had no comment, not keeping up on the latest news. All had heard about some of the states wanting to secede from the union. My thoughts were all men should be free. Spoke to Jan saying will go to our mill and just see how things are going. Jan said will go with you and added will you go back to the city with me to find out more up to the date news. My answer was planning on it, knew you were worried about Joel and Laura Lee.

The mill was running well and quite smoothly. The steam engines turned out a lot more power and did away with a lot of extra shafting from the waterwheels. How things had improved in such a short time. The planner to smoothen the boards and planks were an added bonus. The smooth lumber was a going market in the city. Some that wanted logs sawed didn't have the ready coin. We just would take a part of the logs they brought and would sell in the city. This worked out well for them and us.

The family had already headed back to the city. Henry would be up on the news about the happenings. Jan and I rode our pone's and one extra as pack horse. Mom would always comment why you two don't use a carriage. We just said we enjoy riding and find it just as comfortable as a carriage, with much more freedom. Mom's comment, you two are getting older. Henry had news a war had started at some fort a while back. Also heard the south had driven the Union Army into a mass retreat and panic. This didn't sound very good, most had thought it would be over in a short time. When we got to the city my first visit was to the Colonel's quarters. He was already packed up and was ordered to had East. He had not rushed to tell Joel he would be going with him and his troops East. He had decided to give Joel and Laura Lee time together before moving out. Everything was packed and ready to go including Joel's things he knew Joel would be back his leave was almost up. The Colonel said a day or two would not make any difference. He then asked me if I would be willing to scout for him, telling me I still held the rank of major. Will also upgrade your papers and give you my major insignia's to wear on your collar. You won't need a uniform, dress as you see fit. Really didn't know how to take this. Knew Jan would be upset but would expect it if I decide to do this. When back to the house telling everyone the Colonel was leaving as soon as Joel got back

Told Jan about what the Colonel had said asked me to accompany him and Joel as a scout. Bird I know you will go I am not happy about you for Joel going maybe it will help keep Joel safe.

Was the next day the wedding couple's showed up all agog when they received the news, Joel had to leave immediately. There was a sergeant staying at the house. Henry insisted to inform Joel of his new orders. What a disappointed pair Jan started to cry, Laura Lee came to her saying mom we will get threw this. Bell also teared up, Less acted stunned. Jan then came to me saying I know you will go because of Joel. Jan some consider me too old to be on this type of excursion but if I can help keep Joel safe I will go. Jan said Bird I know but come back safe. You will know when to return.

Joel and I said our goodbyes and headed for the post. The Colonel had everything packed and ready to move out the Colonel upgraded my papers to make sure they were up to date telling me to wear that major emblems on my caller at all times. A scout does not where the Army uniform, if you were to be captured they would not be able to say you are a spy. He also gave me a badge to were on my shirt. When you go into another post they will know you are a major. In short order we headed East. We had a couple of wagons for all the troops gear. This really slowed us down. The next post we came to ask: if we could get a few mules to transport our personal gear. They agreed to let us have two of their six.. The sergeant in charge of the mules and horses, said to me his Colonel had told him to let us have the two mules they were having troubles with. Just shrug and said where are they now. The mules were in separate stalls. Sergeant told me this is the one and he is mean as hell. Will have to beat him to make him do anything. He has already stomped a couple of our boys.

Went to the head of the stall and looked at him and proceeded to talk to him. I would not beat him for any reason. The Sgt. and his orderly both had smirks on their faces reach over and gave him a pat on the neck. Then asked for a brush to brush him down. Got a dish of oats and gave him a feed patting him on the neck. Went into his stall and started brushing him down he Would just turn and look at me. After a while could see the fire was leaving his eyes. Now knew had a good mule. The halter they gave me for him was not a good fit. Took the rein and looped it over his neck and then led him outside. He was one beautiful animal. Could see where he had been beaten. One man came toward us.

My mule stiffened up and I knew he was the one what beaten him I just stepped out in front of the mule and told the Cpl. to leave. He said who the hell do you think you are. The Sgt. had stood back just watching. He then stepped in hollering at the Cpl. he's a major you idiot the Cpl. looked surprised as I repeated for him to leave. The Sergeant apologized saying you're not in uniform so he thought you were a civilian. Then told him was a scout and did not wear a uniform just on my collar and the badge the one on my chest.

Went to the headquarters to see how things were going. The guard stopped me saying the Colonel was busy. I just pointed my collar he then came to attention and saluted and stepped aside. The captain sitting at a desk then asked me what I wanted told him looking for the Colonel the captain. He looked at me questioningly, just reached my collar and showed him my majors insignia. He apologized then informed the others I was here. Cole was a full Colonel the officer running this post was a major like my self. He asked if I had found the two extra mule, nodded a yes was satisfied. We stayed for meal and then moved on. The major had informed us he also had orders to head east. His men were all ground soldiers so they did a lot of walking. Thankfully our men were all Calvary.

Joel would also make a good scout good head at being watchful of his surroundings. We would probably separate. With different assignments.

Our trip to me seem like forever. We finally arrived at camp we were assigned to. Colonel Cole introduce me to the group of officers as a major. He also stated he's the best scout I know of. A few days and Joel was assigned a company. Cole was also moving on another assignment. I was to go to another company that was closer to the line that had been established. Found Joel and I were going to the same place. Another jaunt of a couple of days and we found the company. Joel and I went and reported to the Colonel. When Joel saluted then introduce me as a major Bird. The first thing out of his mouth was he gave the order very belligerent I was to salute him just nodded but did not salute him. He then told me again I was to salute him. Shrug my shoulders saying I'm a scout and do not salute anyone. He just glared at me, my thought was why did they assign a man like this over a lot of men. I turned to leave, he said I didn't release you, he told Joel he was released, Joel saluted and left after Joel left told this Colonel that I wasn't assigned to him. He then said you are now just shrug my shoulders. Then told him need a good man to work with me. He said will line up some men for you to choose from tomorrow. Next morning just waited for him to line up the men. Told Joel to stay out of his way as much as you can he is trouble. The orderly that was assigned to him, after he started to salute and I told him not to. Tell the rest of the men not to salute me either. The enemy will look for ranking and take them out first if possible. Joel had told them also not to salute him. The Colonel's orderly came again to tell us he would be here shortly and to get the men he had told the Sergeant to line up. Joel said these are the worst of the detachments so I'm told. The Colonel showed up with all saluting him walk down the line one man look like a roughneck. The other stood at rigid attention. Walked down the line and turn back walking slowly stopped in front of this man. Looked him in the eye he looked back with a grin. My next words were I think you can beat me up also with a grin. Then asked if he would come with me. He gave a nod then told him to get his gear together he started to go, the Colonel piped up saying he didn't release him. I said I did and said go. The Colonel turned red in the face but didn't argue with me. Then he picked out two other men saying they will go with you also just shrug my shoulders.

Knew would have to be a lot more careful. The Colonel dismissed them to get ready. He then turned to his orderly to get his horse ready. The first man I chose was ready to go. The other two weren't too happy about going they were taking their time. Asked my soon-to-be partner his name. Rob was his answer, told him they call me Bird. I told him think the Colonel was just getting rid of a couple of troubles. Rob said they are couple of scoundrels, then last saying he was not much better. My comment was I know better. Rob's answers thanks. We proceeded to load my mule. Told Rob he has been mistreated and doesn't let too many men near him. Rob saying he's a beautiful animal. When the other two joined Rob and myself my first comment was stay away from my mule. He doesn't like people, tolerates very few. Ones comment I've handle his kind before. My first order from me was to stay away from him, letting them know I meant what I said. Rob looked at me and rolled his eyes with a grin. Didn't need a lead on my mule he followed me any time we were on the move.

Talk to some of the men with Joel found this was a new detachment. Had not been in combat as yet. We moved out that afternoon after finding out one of their scouts had not returned. This information let me know our enemy was not too far away road most of the afternoon found a good spot set up a camp for the night. Told Rob was going to scout on foot, Rob said like to go with you, I welcome him. Told other two not to smoke or build a fire until I get back. Rob and I were gone for about three hours. As we were on our way back could smell pipe smoke and a fire. Told Rob will have to move. Those two didn't heed my orders. The enemy were quite close. When we walked into our camp they were cooking I took water and put the fire out grab their pipes and destroyed them. Told them to pack up we were moving now. Rob and I had not unpacked our things and we were ready to move in minutes could see they were both upset with me but not as much as I with them. Told Rob if you can get on their good side I would appreciate it. Were going to have problems with them. Were too close to the enemy camp. If they have a couple of scouts this is the first thing they will look for. Motion to Rob to mount we were leaving. When they see us mount to leave, they then really scramble not to be left behind. Rob also put on a good act as if he was also upset looked at me and winked. I left with them leaving some of their nonessential stuff behind we may have been safe there but wasn't going to take any chances. This one excursion with Rob found to be an excellent wood s man. We made a camp a mile or more away from the last one made a fire and proceeded to have our meal told Rob wanted to go with me for a night excursion we got out of hearing and he then told me they were planning on killing me and deserting. Rob then said will make sure the rifles don't work. They both had muzzle loaders. Told Rob there's another encampment not far away from us. Were downwind far enough so they will not pick up our smoke.. Rob then said were going to have to do something about these two or they are going to get us killed. They were really angry about you destroying their smokes. That night Rob fixed their muzzle loaders.

He plugged the touch holes of each so the flint would set powder off but not the charge. Was surprised they didn't have better rifles. Next morning advise them to pack up were moving turn my back and heard the click and hiss of powder drop to the ground just in case they did go off. Then stood up with my bow and send an arrow through into his chest. Rob taken out the other one before he could get his rifle up. Rob asked if we bury them My answer was no leave them face down. We have to find a safer spot were still a little too close another few miles in the woods we found us small spring fed pond with good cover. Left my mule there and our gear and decided to travel with the other two horses in tow. Needed a place for them to graze. We came out on a farm and did not see too much activity. Watched for a while, then set the horse's free to graze. Went back to the pond and had our meal and relaxed for the evening. We would pick up our horses and my pony in the morning.

Could see my pony on the other side of the rail fence someone had found them and rounded up our horses. We could hear some talking in the distance told Rob will whistle for my pony he will come and you head back to our camp will meet you there. Went out onto a slight rise and whistled to my pony he came on the run easily clearing the fence. I had just brought my bow with me left my rifle with Rob. When I mounted my pony heard a lot of hollering about six were mounting their horses at the farm house one was on his horse and was on the run after me. Headed my pony for the fence. The man on the horse had a good one he was gaining on me. He he had his rifle and could see he would get a shot off before long. Turned with my bowl as we got close to the fence and let an arrow go just as he was raising his rifle to shoot. My arrow took him in the chest and off his horse he went my pony and myself cleared the fence. Knew from Rob and our roaming there was a woods road and headed for that. The other horse was still following me. Look back saw the other men had open the gate and were now following me up the road. Slowed down and caught the reins of the other horse that was still following me, when into my hiding my tracks and out of sight mode and left the road. Then just rode leisurely to our camp at the pond. Rob was getting there just as I rode up. He looked at me and shook his head saying thought that soldier had you. That was one hell of a shot with that bow. My answer was well we ended up with one heck of a horse. Rob then said your mule welcomed me. He knows a good man no surprise. Let my pony to the pond went into his waist and had his fill with the other horse by his side. We built a small fire for evening meal. Went to the pond to clean up. Rob noticed all my scars saying you been in more than one skirmish I can see that.

Well we got out of another close call. Rob then asked we should move our camp gear again. No was my answer they will not locate my sign did a good job of hiding it. We visited for a while telling about our farm and how well it was doing. He telling me his wife and child had died in childbirth. He just rousted about every since he told me was brought up in the woods. I then change the subject saying we best check out that one detachment. They acted like they were planning an attack on Joel's position. We will leave our horses here and go on foot. We packed up dry provisions and water.

When I got to the camp a scout came in from the direction of our detachment we could tell they were getting ready to move out toward our base. Rob and I hurried back to our pond, left everything and road our horses to our base camp. Found Joel and informed him, will now then tell the colonel. After helping him set his men up. Build small fires as they go out quick they will be watching. After dark set your men up leave there bedrolls as if they are still sleeping. Help Joe set things up as if it were as normal camp. Looked a very good set up. Told Joel they will be attacking in the morning at break of dawn. Will go tell a colonel now, May get into a roughest discussion with him. When up to his quarters the orderly was outside. Told him to go to the latrine. The colonel will be yelling for him and he will want you to shoot me. The orderly grinned saying he could handle it. Went in without saluting them proceeded to tell what was going on. He ignored me saying his scouts had heard nothing. His next words were you salute me. My next words were you would be the last man I would salute and wouldn't do it then. I'm not under your authority. His next words you will salute me. Pulled my knife on my shoulder stepped up and told him if he opened his mouth again I would cut his throat. He shut up I told him and now I'm leaving and if you start yelling i will rush back in and do the job. Left getting on my pony waving to Joel, then he started yelling for his orderly, don't know what happened after that was gone with Rob to check on the enemy's movements. Rob and I were right they were moving in to position for a morning attack. Knew our men were as ready as could be. Rob and I thought they had a very good scout and also knew where to attack from. This time they were in for a heck of a surprise. We didn't engage in the next morning fight. Told Rob will go with my bow and see if I can do that scout in. Told Rob after things calm down will go back and get our gear. Rob joined the fight at a well hidden spot moved around to find their major on a knoll watching the attack. There scout also showed up got close enough to get an arrow off but had to stand up to let an arrow fly and had the second one flying, the scout was hit and went down the major also hit. Someone had spotted me and a shot hit me in the shin knocking me down. Had to crawl back into the wooded area the fight was a disaster for the attackers they were pulling out, two came looking for me. I rolled up against a log covered with moss. When they realize there men were all falling back with a lot of casualties. They left and didn't even come close to where I was. Rob was in a position to see what had happened to me he came out very cautiously. They had pulled out and were gone. Called his name and he came over to me, I was sitting on the log. Told him the slug had hit my leg. My leg was crocked and so knew it was broken. Rob help me back to my horse. Told him will let Joel know. Then we go back to the pond to take care of my leg. Joel was busy they had lost two men and the colonel. The colonel had been shot off his horse. Joel wanted to know if I was going to see an Army surgeon. No I will take care of it. Rob had talked to a few of the men they were all glad they new about the attack ahead of time. We headed out and were on our way back to the pond. On The way back Rob told me the orderly had shot the Colonel he was so scared he had ordered his horse. He had mounted and didn't get far. The orderly said the coward was shot off his horse.

Got to the pond and proceeded to clean my leg. The slug had hit the shin bone breaking the bone had a lot of herbs and healing in my gear mom and Sue and insisted. Instructions were in each packet. There is no slug in my leg but it needed to be set.. Asked Rob to help me set it. Hobble over to a couple of saplings and told Rob to pull my leg straight while I held onto the saplings. Rob understood what I wanted him to do. Rob said he had seen it done after horses kicked a man in the leg. A lot of pain just gritted my teeth. Whittled out a couple of splints. Packed the herbs onto the wound wrapped it up to hold the bone straight. Rob went looking for saplings with a good fork to make crutches. A short while and he was back with a suitable pair. Then told Rob were heading back to the farm. Rob said are you going to release me. Rob you came with me when I asked, would like you to stay with me if you are willing. Rob commented thought you would dismiss me now that you are unable to continue our scouting. He said will be more than glad to stay with you. I hoped you would. We took our time on the way back to the city to Henry's home my mule was now very accustomed to our ways and was a good animal still did not like most people we were into two weeks travel when I felt a bad feeling. Told Rob we have to stop for a while something just happened to one of the family. Then I knew it was Joel. In a little while I told Rob Joel was killed in some fight. Rob being with me for a while knew I could sense things. Told Rob this in my daughter's husband.

Kept track of my leg it was doing well thanks to mom and Sue. We stayed off the main trails wherever we could. Killed game with my bow. We ate quite well thanks to mom and Sue and the Indians teach me what was edible roots and plants. Rob was amazed he knew a lot but I just seem to find enough to always satisfy us. Arrived at the city and headed for the Henry's. Henry's help was glad to see us and were surprised. We headed into the house me on crutches, after taking care of our horses and mule. Told the hostlers should be careful around the mule. He was beaten at one time and didn't like most people. We went into the house through the kitchen. Was early afternoon, one maid was still in the kitchen. We scared heck out of her till she recognized me. Asked where everyone was, in the living room was her answer. Headed into the living room stepped through the door. Jan came to her feet and ran to me and hung on. Laura Lee and Bell's comment was the news we got a few days ago was that you and Joel had been killed. Jan said I knew you were hurt really bad but knew you had survived. Laura Lee and Bell asked if I knew what had happened to Joel.. Joel was okay when I left to come home. Broke my leg had to give up my scouting. Then I took time to introduce Rob to everyone. Told everyone Rob and I were scouting we were fortunate to find out an attack on Joel's position. They were very successful at repelling the attack. That's when I broke my leg. Rob interjected Bird was shot he went down I thought he was killed. The fighting stopped within a very short time. Went up to where the last scene major Bird. He was down but okay. He then whistled for his pony he came on the run. We headed back to our safe spot and reset his leg. We headed here once we had splints on major Bird's leg. Jan then said I want to take a look at your leg. On wrapped and Jan said Bird it looks good no infection and healing well. Laura Lee and Bell both gave me a hug. Then Laura Lee said dad I'm so glad you're back. I will miss Joel and started to cry. She blurted out this damn war. Rob and I both had a good soaking bath Rob was amazed at our water supply and our bathrooms. Jan came in and scrub my back and again checked my leg. she said you have a bunch on the side but it's a firm so it will be okay. Jan also found extra cloths for Rob, he is close to my size not much of problem. Jan asked if Rob was going to have to go back. He's assigned to me and will not release him til his enlistment is up. I will release him then. He's been a hell of a good companion. Then also added he came with me voluntarily when I asked. Jan said Bird how you survive is a wonder, I believe it was a lot to do with your Indian friends teachings. Told Jan would like to head for the farm. I was already packing for us she said. Will you ride in the carriage with me, yes I will. Asked Rob if he would handle the horses an our mule. Rob said with pleasure less than a week was back at the farm. Mom and Sue again were surprised to see me. Mom's words were Bird you always seem to survive somehow. Just relax and told Rob to get familiar with the farm also the sawmill. Mom asked if Rob was still in the Army. Just said he is a sergeant assigned to me for his enlistment I won't release him, the war is taken too many good men. Now will concentrate on our two daughters.

CPSIA information can be obtained
at www.ICGtesting.com
Printed in the USA
BVHW03*1454260618
520094BV00002B/5/P